"You're only trying
to frighten me."

Diane searched his sun-darkened
face—proud, dominant and ruthless.

"We have a proverb," the Sheik said, "if
you save a life you own it. It's ironic
that the life I saved is that of a young
woman who is blood kin to the man I
hate most in my life."

He paused significantly. "I shall keep
you in my tent. When you are looking
less like a rag doll, I shall find out what
your eyes are like when you are
kissed. And if your lips are as soft as
they look."

Diane started to tremble—she could
no longer hope that he was playing
with her.

Suddenly he bared his teeth in a
dangerous smile. "You comprehend
what I have in store for you...?"

Other titles by

VIOLET WINSPEAR
IN HARLEQUIN PRESENTS

Other titles by

VIOLET WINSPEAR
IN HARLEQUIN ROMANCES

Many of these titles, and other titles in the Harlequin
Romance series, are available at your local
bookseller. For a free catalogue listing all available
Harlequin Presents and Harlequin Romances, send
your name and address to:

HARLEQUIN READER SERVICE,
M.P.O. Box 707,
Niagara Falls, N.Y. 14302
Canadian address:
Stratford, Ontario, Canada N5A 6W2

VIOLET WINSPEAR

the sheik's captive

Harlequin Books

TORONTO·LONDON·NEW YORK·AMSTERDAM
SYDNEY·HAMBURG·PARIS·STOCKHOLM

Harlequin Presents edition published November 1979
ISBN 0-373-70824-6

Original hardcover edition published in 1979
by Mills & Boon Limited

CHAPTER ONE

A SUN-SCORCHED land like a boundless lake, one that stretched for countless miles, strewn with great sand-dunes that rose and fell in golden waves. There were strange rock formations and stony tracks littered with boulders thrown up from the seas of time, and great pools of shadow where silence lurked.

A tawny ocean, the westering sun running like flame over the jagged ridges of rock and the towering dunes.

Suddenly in the red sky a hawk appeared, hovering on graceful wings and then plunging down as it caught sight of its prey. The bird settled on a rock and its sharp eyes were fixed upon a figure that stirred feebly in the sand, fingernails digging into the grains as if seeking some kind of security, something to cling to as the girl's eyelids fluttered open and her bleared eyes focused upon the motionless miles of sand all around her.

The vermilion sunset blinded her eyes and a groan escaped from her dry lips as her movements made her aware of her seared skin. Her face, neck and hands were sun-blistered, and her eyelids were so sore it was agony to move them. When she tried to turn her head a knife-like pain cut across her skull and she made a hoarse sound of misery and sank down again, her head upon her arm.

The swarming locusts had caused her horse to bolt. They had invaded the oasis like a dark cloud and had descended upon her before she could take firm control of her horse and gallop away from them.

One of the clicking horrors had dropped down the

neck of her shirt and her panic had transmitted itself to her mount ... but it had been mid-morning when the locusts had struck Fetna, and now the sun was setting and Diane realised that she had lain here in the desert for the best part of the day, ever since she had been tossed from the saddle and had watched helplessly as the horse galloped wildly across the sands, leaving her alone with a wrenched ankle.

When she had tried to walk the pain had been too much to bear. She had bound the ankle with her neck-scarf but still she could only hobble along, until suddenly she had stepped upon a hidden stone and fallen flat upon her face.

Memories of the morning slid through her mind, that invigorating ride to the oasis and the remains of the stone fortress where her grandfather had been stationed with his fierce Spahis, those dashing soldiers of the desert in their great scarlet cloaks and long shining boots, their hawklike faces alert and dangerous beneath the white headrobes.

As a schoolgirl Diane had loved Grandpère's tales of his desert legion and the battles they had fought in this area of the Sahara. Upon growing up she had been unable to resist the compulsion to visit the fortress; she had so wished that Grandpère could travel with her, but he was no longer a fit and able man. His old wounds made a martyr of him these days and he spent most of his time in his garden in Brittany, watering his flowers and writing his memoirs.

'Go and see the old place for me,' he said to Diane. 'But take warning, *chérie*, don't ride to the fortress alone. Do you hear me?'

Diane moved her aching head against her arm ... all might have been well and her visit to Fetna might have been without mishap if she had heeded her grandfather's warning, but the hotel at Dar-Arisi had been filled with the kind of people Diane found tiresome—chattering tourists with their guide books and cameras, and honeymoon couples wrapped up in each other. She had a natural shyness and was always quite happy to be by herself, and choosing a good mount from the stables at Dar-Arisi she had ridden out to Fetna with a water-bottle hooked to the saddle and a small gun in her hip-holster.

It had been so peaceful there, and so alive for her with the stories her grandfather had related ... until that sudden storm of locusts, raining down on the trees and shrubs and everything in sight, including Diane herself.

Oh, what an idiot she had been to lose her head over a beetle down her shirt, but still her skin quivered at the feel of its wings. There in the saddle she had beat at herself until she dislodged the thing, but in her panic she had lost control of the horse and hours had passed while she lay half-baked by the sun, each movement bringing her out in a perspiration that caused her to become parched with thirst. She had drifted finally into a semi-conscious sleep, until the cooling down of the sun had brought her back to reality.

'Never let your nerves get the better of your discipline,' her grandfather always said. 'When you lose your self-control you lose the fight.'

Lost was the word ... Diane knew herself to be miles from Dar-Arisi and hopelessly adrift in the desert, and because she hadn't made any friends at the hotel any concern about her absence would be minimal. Her only hope was that the owners of the hired horse would contact the hotel manager to find out what had become of their property and in so doing arouse interest in what had become of her.

Diane racked her sore head to remember if she had mentioned at the stables that she was going to visit the fortress at Fetna. Somehow she didn't think she had. She had asked for a spirited horse because she was an excellent, well-taught rider, but she hadn't bargained for a descent of locusts.

Dieu, whatever was she going to do? Being the granddaughter of a Frenchman with whom she had lived for the past nine years Diane was inclined to be Gallic in her reactions. She had nerve, but right now she was parched, exhausted, and very unnerved. The Sahara was a vast place and sometimes the only people to be seen on its plains were wandering nomads, scruffy desert dwellers who were often lawless and who would regard a white woman who fell into their hands as fair booty to be sold off in the market, or carried off as a servant into the depths of Timbuctoo.

With his vast knowledge of the desert Grandpère had lectured her upon its manifold dangers. She had solemnly promised him that she wouldn't do anything silly or risky, but the desert air, like an unknown wine, had gone to her head and she had taken that ride to Fetna alone because there had been no one at the hotel with whom she cared to share the experience.

She had wanted to imagine the fortress as it had been when Colonel Philippe Gérard Ronay was there, when the bugles had called his Spahis to their mounts and they had galloped behind him out of the great stone gateway to go and confront the Arabs who wanted to drive the French out of the desert. In her opinion the French colonials had done a great deal to help civilise this tameless land, but their efforts had never been fully appreciated. She knew about the bloodshed, but the army was stationed here to protect the colonists from the Arabs, some of whom could be ruthlessly cruel in their pursuit of freedom from the French administration.

Grandpère had always done his duty in Diane's estimation. A soldier obeyed orders and didn't ask questions.

Diane groaned to herself and wished too late that she had obeyed the Colonel's order. Pride was said to lead to a fall, and here she was the victim of such a fall. Bracing herself against the pain that hammered at her temples, she forced herself to sit up, gasping as the desert sands seemed to spin around her. She gave a cry, which was echoed by the hawk that crouched on a nearby rock, gazing down at her with sharp and curious eyes set above a curving beak. The bird suddenly spread its wings and Diane had the frightened feeling that it was getting ready to swoop down on her. She waved her arms about as if to fend it off, but all at once the hawk wasn't looking at her but was cocking its head as if some other sound had caught its attention.

With a pounding heart, and feeling as if at any moment she would keel over from faintness, Diane watched the hawk spread its wings until they must have measured a span of three feet. It rose into the air and hovered there, then it swooped in a graceful arc above her figure and she felt herself crouching down in self-protection when quite distinctly she caught the sound of a long almost melodic whistle. She heard it three times and realised that it was meant for the hawk. Somewhere out there in the desert the master of the hawk was calling it, and Diane's heart gave an erratic throb. She hardly knew if she was glad or sorry that another human being was in her vicinity. Arabs flew hawks, and whoever was riding this way was bound to be a man of the desert rather than a countryman of her own.

With an exhausted feeling of fatalism Diane sank

down on the sands again. She hadn't the voice to call the
man, she could only wait for him to arrive upon the
escarpment that towered above the place where she lay.

Again across the desert came the sound of his whistling
call to the hawk, who suddenly answered, flying upwards
on graceful wings to hover against the last flaming
colours of the sunset. In that instant several riders appeared on the ridge that ran like a stone spine above
Diane; she saw hazily the outline of horsemen in cloaks
and there was absolutely nothing she could do but lie
there and watch them thread their way down the rocky
incline, stones shifting and rattling beneath the hooves
of the fine-looking horses ... Arabian like the men who
rode them.

As they drew nearer to Diane she noticed that one of
them rode ahead of the others, his great cloak spread
across the hindquarters of his mount, the last rays of the
sun glinting on the spurs at the heels of long red boots. As
he drew nearer to her prone figure he flung some words
over his shoulder and the throaty Arabic consonants sent
a stab of fear through Diane. She watched with dilated
eyes as the hawk flew to him and settled on the wrist of
his gauntlet, and like that he came riding within a few
yards of her figure when he abruptly brought his mount
to a standstill.

He sat there for several moments just looking at her,
as if trying to make up his mind if she were a boy or a
girl. In the deepening dusk she could have been either.
Before she had come to the desert her hair had been cut
into a short page-boy style, and she wore breeches
tailored to her slim hips and a white shirt. To relieve her
twisted ankle she had managed to remove her left boot
and her blue neck-scarf was tied around her ankle. Her
pulses jarred in a most unboyish way when the Arab

suddenly dismounted, settling the hawk on his saddle-bow, from which he unhooked a water-bottle on a strap.

Diane lay there, even more dry-mouthed as he came to her and stood over her, his spurred heels only inches from her head. '*Roumia!*' He flung the word over his shoulder as he suddenly crouched down and began to remove the cap from the water-bottle. '*Mais certaine-ment,*' she heard him mutter in French, his gaze flicking the neck of her shirt and moving down to where her bosom rose and fell in time with her agitated heartbeat. '*Permettez-moi.*' He lifted her across his robed arm and put the rim of the water container to her sore lips. She gulped the liquid thirstily and discovered that instead of water she was drinking cool lemonade, unexpected and utterly delicious.

'Enough!' He drew the rim away from her lips and gazed down intently at her face. 'In a moment or two, *bint*, you may have some more. How come that you are here like this? Where are your companions, eh?'

From comments in French he had spoken suddenly in throaty accented English, as if something about her made him decide that she was of that nationality. Half of her was. From her British mother Diane had inherited Greuze-gold hair and a pair of blue eyes.

'I—I'm alone,' she told the Arab, not realising in her present state of feebleness that such an admission to a stranger was unwise. 'My horse threw me some hours ago a-and my ankle was hurt when I fell—could I please have some more lemonade? I'm so fearfully dry——'

'A condition to be expected if you have lain in the sun for some time.' Again he placed the bottle at her lips and as she drank greedily from it her eyes were fixed upon his face. Even in the dusk his eyes were the most arrest-ing she had ever seen. *Yeux de braise.* The words sprang to her mind. Eyes of fire! As dense as the jagged scar was livid down the side of his hawklike face, almost as deep as if it touched the bone. His headcloth was held in place by double ropes and in the last flare of the sun Diane had noticed that his cloak of heavy rich cloth was royal-blue. The double ropes and the colour of his cloak were insignia of authority, but his face alone would have told her that he was a desert chief.

Wth a sigh she released the water-bottle. Its delicious contents had relieved her parched throat, but her skin still felt as if it had been seared by a flame. Right through her shirt the hot sun had penetrated to her skin, and her ankle throbbed at the slightest movement.

'*Merci*, how I needed a drink! Where exactly am I?' she asked. 'Am I very far from Dar-Arisi?'

'The Pleasure Gardens, eh?' He spoke sardonically. 'That is where you were staying? Your family or friends will be wondering what has become of you.'

'I'm not with my family——' Abruptly Diane bit her lip and winced at the jab of pain. This man was an Arab and here she was foolishly telling him that she had no relatives at Dar-Arisi to be concerned about her. She gathered her wits, scattered as they were in her aching head. 'Yes, my friends will definitely be wondering about me—can you possibly take me to the hotel? I'd be most grateful——'

'I'm not a porter, *bint*.' His arrogant eyes swept her from head to foot. 'You must have very good friends if they allow you to ride in the desert alone, and you must be an excellent horsewoman if you fall off in the middle of nowhere and get yourself a sunburn that will feel like hell in the morning. Come, you had best spend the night at my *douar*.'

'*Douar?*' she echoed, the frightened thump of her heart

almost knocking the breath from her throat.

'My encampment.' His voice was deep and deliberate, with a sensual resonance to it. 'Night has fallen and I have no intention of leaving you here, a prime target for the brutes who hunt in the dark. What is the matter, *bint*? Don't you like the idea of being invited to my tent? Does it strike you as more dangerous than being left here in the desert to face the night alone?'

'I—I don't know you!' She spoke nervously. 'You obviously know Dar-Arisi and I don't think it would inconvenience you all that much to take me there.'

'My men and I have been hunting all day and we're tired and hungry for our supper, added to which, young English Miss, I don't take orders from a mere girl. You will do as I say!'

'I—I'm not one of your lackeys to be spoken to like that!' she said indignantly. 'Who do you think you are?'

'Caid of the Beni-Haran.' He made an imperious gesture with his whip. 'I am the Sheik Khasim ben Haran and you are in my territory, the desert of Shemara. That being so you are a guest of the Beni-Haran and not a delectable female I am carrying off to enjoy as dessert to my supper. No doubt your head is filled with tales of barbaric Bedouins who find white girls irresistible, but in your present state of sunburn, with sand grits in your hair, you are hardly a threat to my libido. I assure you, *bint*, if you are concerned about your chastity, then dismiss the notion. It's absurd!'

'Thanks!' Her burned skin tingled as the blood rushed to her cheeks. As the granddaughter of a distinguished French officer she had always been protected from harsh encounters with men, but right now she was in no doubt that she was in the company of a man to whom girls were either playthings or servants. A Caid was a desert chief of high authority, but a warning whispered in her brain that above all he was an Arab to whom women were as much sport as any gazelle or sand cat.

'Come, we must be on our way! Place your arms about my neck, *bint*, and I shall hurt you less when I lift you.'

There was nothing Diane could do but obey his order, but she couldn't suppress a gasp of pain as she raised her sunburned arms and encircled his neck with them.

'When we reach the *douar* my servants will provide treatment for your blisters,' he said, and holding her as if she weighed no more than a young animal he strode to where his horse awaited him with a restless jingling of its harness. Diane was placed upon the saddle and when the Sheik mounted behind her, he wrapped a fold of his cloak around her. The night had grown suddenly cold and Diane was shivering and a tired compliance had come over her. She was in this man's hands, a *fait accompli*, and to submit was less exhausting than trying to persuade him to take her to Dar-Arisi tonight. He was obviously the sort who didn't change his course once it was set.

She heard him speak in Arabic to his men and the only word she understood was *roumia*, which meant foreign woman. He was no doubt telling them what had happened to her, and as his horse began to lope across the sands he drew her tired, aching body against him and Diane's head felt so heavy that it seemed to rest against his shoulder of its own volition. She could smell horse leather on his robes, *cigarro* smoke of a strong kind, and the warm tang of his skin. Masculine aromas she associated with Grandpère, so that in her helpless tiredness she was less alarmed than she might have been.

She dozed against the muscular shoulder but never

quite lost her awareness that she was being taken by an
Arab to his desert encampment. She wasn't being abducted, she assured herself. The Caid would give her
some supper and see that she was cared for, then in the
morning he would no doubt have her escorted back to
the hotel. This was just an adventure, but one she
wouldn't relate to her grandfather. He wouldn't find it
amusing to be told that she had fallen into the hands of
an Arab. Such men as this one had been the enemy as
far as he was concerned. He had admired their reckless
courage, but that hadn't stopped him from raising his
sabre in defence of the Gallic planters and their families.
Diane well knew that Grandpère had followed the desert
law of an eye for an eye, a tooth for a tooth.

The motion of the horse rocked her to the edge of
sleep, the jingle of harness like a strange lullaby. When
the horse came to a standstill her eyes fluttered open and
she found that the Sheik and his retinue had arrived
among the campfires and the hair tents of the *douar*.

With a lithe economy of movement the Sheik swung
himself to the ground and reached for Diane. '*Ne vous
derangezpas,*' he murmured as his strong arms enclosed
her. He knew that her sun-scorched body had developed
an almost unbearable soreness and so she did as he told
her and lay quite still in his arms as he carried her across
the firelit compound towards a large tent, whose flap a
servant in a white turban and tunic held open for him.
Words in Arabic were exchanged, and Diane noticed even
in her weariness the intonation of authority when the
Sheik switched to his own language. When he spoke in
French his voice seemed to take on a rough-velvet quality,
and the thought stirred through her mind that he probably used the Gallic tongue when he made love to a
woman.

Then as if the thought had to be escaped Diane let her gaze travel around the *grande* tent, for there was no other way to describe it. Its cloth walls matched the colour of the Sheik's cloak, they were royal-blue and hung with the kind of rugs that could only have come from Shiraz, so gorgeous was the intermingling of shades and patterns. Underfoot the carpets had a thick pile and large cushions were spread upon a broad ottoman beside which stood a low inlaid table. A carved box, a lighter and ashtray stood on the table and Diane had an image of the Sheik stretched out upon the ottoman, a *cigarro* between his lips, and a girl kneeling at his side on the carpet, gazing at him with her eyes painted to resemble those of the gazelle, clad in something transparent, with golden bangles on her wrists, and belled chains about her ankles.

'I'm light-headed,' Diane thought distractedly, for it wasn't like her to have notions out of a novelette about passion in the desert. Grandpère had once told her that Arabs loved their horses far more than they loved their women. Horses and hunting, fighting and falcons, he had said, and Diane remembered how the Sheik's hunting hawk had flown ahead of his horse as they rode through the desert to the *douar*. Now the bird had vanished, presumably to its perch for the night.

The tent flap fell in place behind the Sheik's servant as he departed and with care Diane was set upon her feet. She flinched as her left foot touched even the softness of the carpet. 'Razouk is arranging for a girl to come and attend you.' The dark eyes swept Diane from head to foot, seeing her more clearly in the lamplit tent.

Diane returned his gaze, unhappily aware of how unkempt and unattractive she must look with her face reddened from its exposure to the sun, her hair lank and gritty with sand. In contrast the Caid of the Beni-Haran looked in perfect command of himself, the flowing cloak enhancing his lean and haughty carriage. He was very much a part of the oriental strangeness of the great tent; its dusky corners, rich drapes, and mingled aromas of leather, smoke and cassia oil in the lamps that hung from the tent pole. He had, Diane thought, a kind of barbaric grandeur ... the scar down his face could have been inflicted in some desert skirmish, perhaps with a tribal enemy.

He regarded her with a sardonic tilt to the eyebrow above his scar, as if he divined her thoughts about him. His eyes made Diane think of coal with a flame at the centre; they had a startling density where cruelty or passion could be smouldering. Diane didn't know a great deal about men, but she suspected that this one would shake a woman very thoroughly if he thought she deserved it, and then in a warmer mood pull her down upon his divan and present her with a casual but no doubt costly gift.

In the silence of the look they shared Diane felt the atmosphere become charged with a force which seemed elemental ... as if a storm were coming. Her heart beat heavily and nerves vibrated under her skin, symptoms which could have been caused by her physical exhaustion yet which she felt were due mainly to the personality of the Sheik. Her hand travelled nervously to her shirt opening where her fingers clenched the gold locket which hung there on a neck chain. She trifled with it in a restless fashion, until suddenly the chain came undone and the locket fell to the floor.

Instantly the Sheik retrieved it and as if curious sprang the little lock which opened it. He stared at the picture inside and Diane heard him catch his breath as he stared at the picture, that of a French officer in braided kepi and uniform, a wing of his scarlet cloak flung across his shoulder.

'Who is this man?' The Sheik's black brows slanted together as he rapped out the question and Diane felt her nerves give a jolt when she saw how his dark eyes glittered ... so dark in contrast to the sudden lividity of his scar.

'My grandfather——' The dryness of her throat seemed to increase and the words seemed to scrape past her smarting lips.

'Colonel Philippe Gérard Ronay?' The deep voice cracked like a whip.

'Yes—my grandfather,' she repeated, and was chillingly aware that danger had slid into the tent as if it were a snake.

'Your name is Ronay?'

'Diane Claire Ronay,' she replied, and watched wideeyed as he clenched his fist around the locket as if to try and crush it. The deep facial scar stood out against his sun-darkened skin and if eyes could be said to burn his were burning furiously in that moment.

'May I have my locket?' she gasped. 'You'll damage it——'

'I should like to damage the man whose likeness is inside!' He snarled the words and then in an access of fury he flung the locket at Diane's feet. 'That man was a pitiless enemy of my people! He destroyed them without mercy—my mother among them!'

Diane's eyes filled with horror at his words. 'Grand-père was a soldier—I refuse to believe that he ever killed a woman.'

'I won't be called a liar by you, *bint*!' In a stride the Sheik was across the tent and a hand closed cruelly on

Diane's shoulder, grinding into the fine bones as if he meant to crush them to powder. She winced at the pain and gazed up fearfully into eyes aflame with hostility; a vein beat at his temple and she could feel the violence barely held in check. A whimper of fear escaped her, for never had she seen such menace in a man's face, as naked and threatening as if a sword was raised against her. She flung up a hand as if to shield herself against him, and as he saw the gesture his lips twisted and he flung her away from him so she stumbled and fell to the floor.

'That's what my mother did, raised a hand in the pathetic hope of protecting herself,' he said harshly.

Diane shuddered, for how could she believe such a thing of that tall, stooped figure working upon his memoirs in the lovely old Breton garden filled with the scent of roses and the sea? 'You're mistaken,' she said huskily. 'Grandpère couldn't do such a thing——'

'I could never forget that accursed man!' The Sheik stood menacingly over Diane. 'He ordered his Spahis to attack a Beni-Haran encampment and I saw my mother cut down by a sabre. I ran to her and my face was slashed to the bone by the steel that was running with her blood!'

Diane caught her lip painfully between her teeth, for she knew from her grandfather's memoirs that he had fought the Arabs relentlessly, especially upon an occasion when an entire family of French colonials had been massacred and his Spahis had retaliated without mercy.

'Your people are just as cruel to the French,' she said defensively.

'My people are the Beni-Haran, and they aren't cruel without justification!' His teeth seemed to bite out the words. 'I always swore I would get even with Colonel Ronay—he is still alive?'

'Yes, but long retired from the army.' Diane's eyes were fixed nervously upon the Sheik's stony face. 'Y-you can't mean to hurt an old man?'

'An old man, no!' He spoke contemptuously and was gazing intently at Diane. 'I imagine that if Ronay has it in him to care for anyone, he cares for you, eh? Is he staying at Dar-Arisi?'

'No——' She caught her breath as her heart throbbed. 'He's a long way from North Africa—a long way from you!'

'Unlike his granddaughter!' The Sheik abruptly reached for her and jerked her upright, grasping her by the chin in such a way that she couldn't move a muscle of her face and had to suffer his hard-eyed scrutiny. 'I suppose you listened to his stories of the desert and had to see for yourself if the place was as fascinating as he described it? Mmm, I expect when you are bathed and not looking like a boiled lobster you are quite a present-able *bint*. I am aware that the French protect their young women in much the same way as we protect ours, so I am taking a guess that you are still quite innocent where men are concerned. Am I correct?'

Weary and aching as she was Diane felt an impulse to fight back and not show this Arab that the touch of his hand and the implication in his words had tied a knot of fear inside her. Never before had she felt such apprehension, not even when she had lain in the hot sun and felt as if she were being slowly grilled. As tormenting as that had been, it had not been related to this far more primitive fear in the shape of a man.

'I came to Dar-Arisi with a chaperone,' she lied. 'A search party will be looking for me right now, so you—

you'd be well advised to have me escorted to the hotel before they find me here——'

'A chaperoned young woman wouldn't be riding alone in the desert. I'm the leader of a people who can spin the most colourful tales, *bint*, and I know you are spinning one right now. There are no friends searching for you, no one knows where you are, and after a day or two and you fail to return to Dar-Arisi it will be assumed that you have perished of sunstroke and thirst in the desert. No doubt by then camel riders will be sent out officially to search for you or your remains; if they find none they will take the view that animals have dragged your body to their lair. They do this, you know, often saving a carcase so they can enjoy it at nightfall.'

Diane shuddered and could feel such a weakness in her body that she longed to sink down on to the ottoman and just give way to misery and helplessness. But that would please him. He wanted to make her curl up with terror.

'You don't know my grandfather,' she said defiantly. 'He won't give up until I'm found—he knows the desert and the kind of men who live in it.'

'Then if he knows the desert, *bint*, and the kind of man that I am, he'll be aware that by the time you are found you will no longer be the proud young innocent who came here, beguiled by the romantic tales of a Colonel of Spahis.'

In her weary state it took a moment or two for his meaning to sink into Diane's mind; her deep sense of shock was delayed for several seconds, and then she cast a wild glance at the tent flap and forgetful of her wrenched ankle made an attempt to run past the Sheik. Pain crippled her and even as she felt herself falling, arms caught hold of her and she was swung off her feet and carried to the ottoman.

'Fate,' he mocked, 'has seen to it that you are helpless in my hands. We Arabs believe in Kismet, you know, and for a long time I've craved to punish Colonel Philippe Ronay. Because I had the Beni-Haran to consider I couldn't go after him with a gun, but now thanks to Kismet I can hurt him in a way that no bullet ever could. A bullet in the brain is too quick, but he'll suffer the torments of the damned when he learns that his beloved granddaughter has fallen into the hands of one of his Arab enemies from the old days. He will not be informed of my name, of course, but as he made countless enemies here in the desert he will be able to take his choice. It truly amazes me that he allowed you to visit this part of the world. Has he grown senile in his retirement?'

At this additional insult Diane had to strike back, but his reflexes were swift and he caught her by the wrist before her hand met his face, making her gasp as she felt the bruising strength of his grip.

'So you like to fight, eh?' His teeth glinted against his skin in a taunting smile. 'I'm bored by tame things myself, *bint*, but right now you are in no fit state for the kind of match I have in mind.'

Diane gazed at his mocking face and the meaning in his words suddenly struck through her and she flinched away from him. Since the age of eleven she had lived a sheltered life with her grandfather, who had removed her from her convent school when her parents were killed in a Swiss avalanche. He had educated her with the assistance of a French governess. She had been kept away from boys, perhaps to compensate for the way the Colonel's son had married while still a student, taking for his wife an English chorus girl, Grandpère had never forgiven Raoul, her father, for marrying so irresponsibly, and he hadn't seemed to notice that in recent years Diane had grown to look very much like her mother, with a bright shine to her hair and long slender legs.

Diane knew that he had taken it for granted that she preferred his company to that of young people. His guardianship had been careful but never severe, and when she had asked him if she could visit North Africa he had seemed pleased that she should want to see the places where he had spent many years as a cavalry officer.

'The desert can be mysterious and beautiful,' he had said, 'but never take it for granted. Give me your word you'll take care of yourself and I'll permit you to go there. I would like you to have the experience. There is nothing on earth to equal a desert sunset, or kebab cooked in a fire on a naked sword.'

But the guests at Dar-Arisi had bored her with their gossip and their tea-dances and she had broken her word to Grandpère. He had trusted her to do as he asked and if she had obeyed him she wouldn't be here in the encampment of an Arab; she'd be at the hotel, preparing to dine with people whose innocuous company would have been welcome right now. Their chatter would have been music in her ears, but instead she heard the barbaric sound of Arabic speech beyond the tent walls.

Her self-will and pride had led her into this predicament, yet still in some innocent part of her brain she harboured the hope that Khasim ben Haran was only playing with her. He was a man of responsibility, a tribal leader, so he couldn't really mean what he implied.

'I—I believe you're only trying to frighten me.' She searched his sun-darkened face and dared the eyes which held a brazen gleam deep inside their darkness. He straightened up and looked both powerful and temperamental as he stood there in his great cloak. Each feature of his face was as if carved by the artisans whose work had survived in the stone friezes of sandstone tombs; the hawklike profile of the desert chiefs, proud, dominant and ruthless.

'We have an old Arabic proverb,' he said, 'to the effect that if you save a life, you own it. It's ironic that the life I should save is that of a young woman who is blood kin of the man I hate most in my life. Destiny has spun this web you are caught in, for when I set out this morning to hunt in the desert with my men I little dreamed that I would find a stricken gazelle who has the misfortune to bear the brand of my greatest foe. Some men would kill you for this, but I am a little more civilised than they are, just a little more appreciative of sapphire eyes and a soft pair of lips.' He paused, significantly. 'I shall keep you in my tent, I think, and when you are looking less like a rag doll I shall find out what your eyes are like when you are kissed, and if your lips are as soft as they look.'

As his words sank slowly into Diane's dazed mind she felt fear of him stab through her body. Her gaze ran wildly around the tent, but she knew despairingly that there was no escape from him while her ankle was so useless. She could barely hobble, let alone run, and this Arab was as strong and agile as a sand leopard. He could bring her down and do as he pleased with her, and the one person who cared what became of her was miles away in Brittany.

She started to tremble ... she could feel the tremor in her knees and even inside her. Always there had been Grandpère to comfort and guide her, and now there was nobody.

Nobody but the Sheik Khasim ben Haran who stood regarding her without a vestige of sympathy in his eyes ... eyes that raked over her as if assessing how she would look when the effects of sunburn had worn off.

Suddenly he bared his teeth in a dangerous smile. 'You comprehend what I have in store for you, otherwise I'll explain in more detail.'

'You don't need to give me any detailed descriptions of what a woman can expect when she falls into your clutches,' Diane said stormily. 'One look at you tells me all I need to know about your attitude towards women— even if I weren't a Ronay I doubt if I'd escape unmolested from your hands!'

'My Arab hands?' He showed them, lean and leathered as his riding whip, reaching out as if to take her by the neck. 'If you've had details of what Arabs do to white women, then what were you doing riding alone in the desert? Perhaps you were looking for an amorous encounter with one of my kind, eh? A brown-skinned barbarian who would throw you to the sands and be less polite than your hand-kissing Frenchmen?'

'Such a thought never entered my head,' she said furiously. 'I should hope I've more sense than to behave like a frustrated nitwit out of a novelette!'

'You weren't exactly using your wits, *ma fille*, when you rode out alone from your hotel.'

'No,' she agreed. 'My common sense should have warned me that there are jackals in the desert.'

'Women always feel the need to be insulting when they're frightened.'

'I'm not cowering at your knees in fright.' Diane looked at him with all the scorn she could muster, and wished fervently that her own knees weren't shaking as she stood up to face him. *Dieu*, never had a man looked so tall and menacing, and so capable of carrying out his threats. There was about him from head to heel an untamed masculinity that had long since been bred out of city men. She couldn't imagine him anywhere but in the desert, cloaked and robed, and tawny as its sands.

'What holds you up, willpower?' Deliberately he moved a step closer to her, the spurs chiming at his booted heels. Diane couldn't prevent herself from backing away from him, gasping as the backs of her knees came in contact with the ottoman and made her lose her balance. She fell down weakly and shrank away as the Sheik leaned a knee upon the side of the ottoman and looked at her in mocking silence.

A scarred and deadly stranger she had been destined to meet . . . as the moth meets the beckoning flame.

'Don't——' It was almost a whisper and she defensively fixed her eyes upon his scar as if it repulsed her . . . the truth was that it was his dangerous-looking mouth which made her feel limp with fear. She had an image of those lips crushing her own, kissing her as a man kissed a woman, with the hunger and urgency of male appetite.

'What mustn't I do?' His eyes taunted her with his awareness that she was at his mercy, and they both knew he was merciless as the Spahi who had driven cruel steel into his mother. 'Have you not told me, *bint*, that I am an Arab who has only a single use for women? That being the case, then why waste your breath to plead with me?'

'I—I'm not pleading with you——'

'Aren't you? I could have sworn I saw such a look in your eyes.'

'I wouldn't lower myself to plead with you!'

'I wouldn't listen to your pleas even if you crawled on your hands and knees,' he rejoined.

'I'd sooner die than crawl to you!'

'I believe you almost mean that, *bint*.' He scanned her sun-seared defiant face. 'It rather pleases me that I have a skirmish on my hands rather than a whimpering surrender. If you gave in too readily I'd be robbed of the pleasure of defeating you.'

'Is that how you get your pleasures, by beating women?'

'Not with my whip,' he taunted. 'My weapons are a trifle more subtle and most effective.'

'Your kisses would make me ill.' She flung the words in his face. 'I suppose that's what you're referring to?'

'Kisses—and more,' he said insinuatingly. 'If you weren't so sunburned and straggly I'd give you a sample right now.'

At his words temper and terror flared together in her eyes. 'I—I feel sorry for the Beni-Haran having a cruel brute like you in charge of them. 'It's a pity that sabre didn't find your cold heart instead of your face——'

'You will cease what you are saying!' Suddenly a look of bitter anger ravaged his scarred face and uncaring that her shoulders were sore even through her shirt he gripped them with his hands and shook her so her head tossed back and forth on her aching neck.

'You're a Ronay right enough!' He spoke cuttingly, his eyes like black steel as they raked down her body. 'And if I were as cruel as you believe, I'd take you right now and torture your skin with my touch until you screamed for mercy. You would feel as if you were being flayed alive—do you want that?'

'I'm beyond caring,' she gasped. 'I know already that by the time I get out of your clutches I shall wish myself dead!'

'Then so be it!' He flung her away from him and stood to his full height, impressively above the normal for a man who looked every inch an Arab. The desert was stamped into his features ... the Orient burned in his dark eyes ... the need to exact vengeance beat at the Eastern heart of him.

Diane lay where he had flung her, gazing up wordlessly at his cloaked figure, seeing her fate there in his eyes.

She couldn't look away from him ... she felt as trapped and seared as a moth in a flame.

CHAPTER TWO

ABRUPTLY the tall cloaked figure swung on his heel and swept open the tent flap. He spoke to someone, who then entered while he departed. A young Arabian girl came towards Diane, half-veiled and carrying a first-aid box in her hands. She was followed by the white-clad servant who carried a large copper bowl filled with water; he went on past Diane, towards a section of the tent that was covered by a scarlet hanging. He took the bowl in there and then reappeared. Diane felt him looking at her, then he said something to the girl in the language that sounded so barbaric to Diane's ears. To her relief the girl addressed her in French.

'Achmed says that the *sitt* requires clothing but there is nothing of European style that he can provide. Would the *sitt* mind if he brought her an Eastern outfit?'

Diane glanced down at her own clothes and saw how

crumpled and dirty they were; she longed for something fresh to wear and wouldn't have cared right now had these people provided her with a sheet to wrap around her.

'Please tell Achmed that I shall be pleased to wear whatever he brings me. Will you ask him if my own clothes can be cleaned and pressed as soon as possible?'

The girl turned to Achmed and related what Diane had said. He inclined his turbaned head and left the tent, and with a tired feeling of compliance Diane submitted to the girl's attentions. A soothing greasy lotion was rubbed gently into the skin of her face, the slim fingers working it in carefully so the skin wouldn't break. 'There will be some peeling on the forehead and nose,' the girl murmured, 'but in about a day the *sitt* will feel less sore.'

'*Merci*, you are very kind.' Diane studied what she could see of the girl's face; the veil covered her lower features, but her large brown eyes were visible, doe-like eyes beneath intricately looped plaits of very dark hair. Through the veiling Diane glimpsed the glistening gem that studded one of the girl's nostrils. She wore a flowered tunic over pantaloons and there was a scarab on a chain about her neck.

'Come, if the *sitt* will wash, then I can apply the lotion to other parts which have been sunburned, and I can bind up the ankle.'

'I'd love a wash.' Diane rose unsteadily to her feet and was assisted into the section of the tent where Achmed had placed the bowl of water on a mat. Diane was too weary, too emotionally shaken by her encounter with Khasim ben Haran to make any protest when her shirt was unbuttoned and removed, the belt of her breeches unlatched, along with the fastenings of her brassiere. She allowed herself to be sponged in cool water from her neck to her throbbing ankle, not unaware that the Arabian girl's eyes had widened at the whiteness of her skin where the sun hadn't reached. Diane had very white skin inherited from her mother, and long slim legs which tapered to fine-boned ankles. Her hips and derriere were almost boyish in their slenderness, but her bosom had an impertinent curve to it. She couldn't help but feel rather self-conscious to have someone bathing her. At the convent school the girls had bathed in cubicles and were obliged to wash beneath a white garment which concealed their nudity from their own gaze as well as that of anyone else.

'The *sitt* is very slim in the thighs.' The Arabian girl smiled at Diane. 'But such pretty breasts make up for the lack of plumpness elsewhere.'

The remark startled Diane; she had no close female friends and was unused to the way girls compared their figures and remarked openly on each others good points.

Diane glanced down at herself, shuddering at the boiled look of her neck, arms and hands in contrast to the rest of her body. 'I look awful,' she gasped. 'Like a patchwork!'

'The redness will fade. I expect already that the *sitt* is feeling less sore—it was a fortunate thing that my lord the Sheik Khasim found you and was able to bring you here to his *douar*. European people don't always realise the hazards of the desert, they see only its enchantment, whereas we who are part of it are more aware of its dangers. To be lost in the desert and not found is a terrible fate.'

More terrible, Diane wondered, than falling into the hands of a man who had reason to hate a woman because her name was Ronay?

'Is the Sheik Khasim a very ruthless man?' she asked.

'He is all-powerful to the men of the Beni-Haran. They respect his authority and admire his strength and courage.'

'What of the women?' Diane couldn't help feeling curious. 'What do they think of him?'

'They would like the honour of being his *kadine* and having a child from him, preferably a son who would ensure her security.'

'Isn't he married?' Diane drew around her the folds of a big Turkish towel, so soft in texture that it was kind to her skin. 'I thought men of his position had at least four wives, not to mention a harem filled with girls.'

'The Sheik Khasim takes his time about selecting his wives, but there is, of course, a harem at the *kasbah*. Over the years he has been given gifts of women by the chiefs of other tribes, some of whom he has married off to his officers.'

'What an honour!' Diane's lips twisted scornfully. 'After he has finished with them he passes them on like used clothing!'

'Oh, but you are quite wrong.' The Arabian girl looked appalled by Diane's remark. 'My lord Khasim would not dally with a woman unless he meant to keep her, and it is well known among the Beni-Haran that he gives only virgin brides to his men. A girl no longer a virgin would not be a suitable wife for any Arab, whether he has a high or low position in life. A girl must remain untouched by a man so that on her wedding night the bed sheet will show the signs of her chastity. This sheet is hand-embroidered by a bride and is shown to her husband's family the morning after he has made love to her.'

'How primitive!' Diane sat on a divan, the big towel draped around her while her ankle was bound with a crêpe bandage.

'It is the law of the desert.' The girl gave Diane a curious look. 'Is it different among your people, *sitt*? Does it not matter to a European man if a girl has lain with other men before her marriage?'

'It has become a rather outmoded custom in some European countries,' Diane admitted. 'But I must say that in France it's still considered proper for a girl to keep her chastity.'

'I believe the *sitt* herself is still a virgin.' The brown eyes above the veil gazed impudently at Diane. 'You would not be so shy of being seen unclothed if you had lain with a man.'

Diane felt a tingling blush beneath her sun-scorched skin; if it was evident to this girl that she was so basically innocent, then it must have been even more evident to the man who had swept his dark eyes over her and threatened her innocence in a way that made her toes curl. She had a mental image of him in that great cloak, his ox-blood boots fitting close to his long legs, the glint of steel at his heels. A man who ruled an entire tribe of Arabs would have no qualms about taming a girl and making her submit to his demands. He could do as he liked with her and there wasn't a person in this encampment who would question his autocracy, especially with regard to a female.

With gentle, honey-coloured hands the Arabian girl applied the soothing lotion to Diane's legs and arms and wherever else the sun had burned her.

'What's your name?' Diane asked her.

'Yasmina, which is Arabic for jasmine flower.'

'It's very pretty and suits you.' Her soothed skin eased Diane's tension, and for a while, at least, she could relax in the knowledge that she was no longer lost in the desert and at the mercy of its elements. Here at the

Sheik's *douar* she was being cared for, and if she could keep him at arm's length she might enjoy certain aspects of this strange misadventure.

'The *sitt* is kind to say so.' Yasmina smiled and took from a nearby table a tortoiseshell hairbrush initialed with the letter K. She began to apply it to Diane's hair, carefully brushing out the sand grains and stroking back some of the shine. Diane let her gaze wander around the sleeping section of the big tent; the mellow-tinted rugs glimmered in the lamplight, and across the broad low bed lay a cover with the lustre of a peacock's tail. The few items of furniture were intricately carved, and she noticed several pairs of riding-boots on leather jacks, and some books on the bedside table beside a copper lamp. The tent wall at the back of the bed was hung with colourful, tasselled harness-covers. The lamps emitted a spicy scent, not strong but constant.

This was where the Sheik slept, sprawled on the ottoman amid its barbaric surroundings.

'I will see if Achmed has left clothing for the *sitt*.' Yasmina went into the main part of the tent. Diane stood up to try her ankle, but was so physically weak that before she could save herself she had toppled on to the bed and was lying there, barely covered by the towel, when someone far taller and more intimidating than Yasmina stepped into the sleeping apartment.

He stood there looking down at Diane, his dark eyes moving over her with deliberation. 'Were you expecting me?' he drawled.

Diane lay there in a state of shock, gazing up at the Sheik, who was clad in a dark kaftan over tight-legged trousers. He had discarded his headcloth and his hair was like sable, cut close to his head except for a truant strand across his brow. Here the lamplight muted his scar and

Diane saw how good-looking he would have been if the left side of his face had not been so badly cut about ... a sabre slash which had driven to the bone. As if reading her thoughts he turned his face into the light and Diane couldn't stop herself from flinching.

'How are you feeling now?' he asked. 'Yasmina tells me she has bathed you and attended to your ankle.'

'I—I feel much easier.' Diane struggled to sit up and immediately he extended a hand and drew her into a sitting position.

'But weak as a kitten from lack of food, eh? That will be remedied, but first you had better put these on.' He held out some garments in his other hand. 'Do you need assistance?'

'No, I can manage perfectly well.' Diane gathered the folds of the towel around her and gave him a suspicious look. He was no doubt mocking her, but she couldn't be absolutely sure of a man who had a harem of women and had long since uncovered all the female mysteries. 'I'd be grateful for some privacy, Sheik Khasim. I—I'm not accustomed to an audience while I dress.'

'Come, you need not be coy with me.' He dropped the garments on to the bed at her side. 'I'm aware that girls are different from boys.'

'No doubt,' she flared. 'I've been informed that you have a large harem, but I'm not a member of it!'

'Not yet, *bint*, but your membership is guaranteed.'

Diane caught her breath at the audacity of his remark ... when she looked at him she couldn't ignore the primal warnings that stirred deep inside her. Waves of alarm that beat against the walls of her body.

'Ruthless men, *bint*, know exactly what other men are capable of, and so your grandfather would have been a prudent guardian of a young girl.' A soft laugh issued from the brown throat in the opening of the kaftan. 'I venture to say that you've been kept as secluded as a young nun behind high walls, but now the dove is out of the nest and the hawk has you in his cage.'

A shiver ran through Diane at the vivid analogy and she felt herself shrinking away from the hard masculine strength of the Sheik, and from the scar that constantly reminded him of what had happened before she was even born. 'I can't be held responsible for what happened—it just isn't fair!'

'It's strangely just.' He narrowed his eyes to a dangerous glitter. 'I want Colonel Philippe Ronay to suffer as I did when I held my dying mother in my arms and saw the light of life fade from her eyes. I swore that one day I would make him pay for all that blood, all those tears, and what a refined weapon for my purpose in the shape of his own flesh and blood. It will be arranged that he believes you to be in the unwashed hands of a bearded brute whose sensual appetite matches his greed for a greasy *couscous*. Your grandfather will be unaware that you are actually in the hands of the Caid of the Beni-Haran.'

'Do you regard yourself as a cut above a bearded brute?' asked Diane, scorn and nerves shaking her voice.

'I do wash regularly, *bint*, and I don't guzzle my food from a dish swimming in semolina and grease.'

Diane shuddered. 'Grandpère is now an old man. He's all the family I have—please, won't you be lenient just this once? What pleasure will it give you——?'

She broke off, all at once aware of the Sheik's gaze upon her bare shoulder where the towel had slipped. Her skin burned at her own naïveté. She was a young female, untried and not unattractive. She could provide this man with more than the satisfaction of vengeance ... she glanced hastily away from his tall figure and the sun-tanned hands that were biding their time until he could touch her without making her cry with pain. They weren't coarse hands, she had to admit that to herself, but well-shaped and lean-fingered, the right one bearing a ring incised with a design which was probably Arabic.

She felt the nerves of tension hammering at her temple and wondered how on earth she was going to get away from this place. She felt trapped and couldn't bear to think of Grandpère's reaction when he heard that she had been abducted by an Arab who fiercely hated him. Grandpère would blame himself for letting her travel to the desert. Such worry and anxiety could have a dis-astrous effect on his health.

'I—I suppose you'll be satisfied if you cause my grand-father to be ill?' she said. 'He's old and he isn't strong any more, and I know he regrets some of the things he had to do when he was a soldier.'

'I regret that I've had to wait this long to get even with him.' The Sheik suddenly reached down and taking Diane's hair in his fist he forced her to look up at him. 'Our desert law says that we take an eye for an eye, a tooth for a tooth. I shall take all of you, *bint*, piece by piece, but first I shall want something from you that will convince your grandfather that I have you.'

The dark eyes raked over her and settled on the slim gold bangle on her wrist, which had a little jade monkey attached to it. 'Did he give you that?'

'No——' The bangle had belonged to her mother and had been Raoul Ronay's first present to her.

'Nonetheless he will know it is yours. Take it off!'

'I shan't——'

'Then I'll take it off for you.' Hard fingers took her by the wrist and even as she struggled with him, he held her effortlessly with his left hand while he found the catch of the bangle and removed it. He studied the little monkey for a few moments, while Diane gazed up at his strong scarred face and hated him so much that it made her tremble.

'You brute!' she gasped. 'I suppose you're well used to making women do as you want?'

He gave her a withering look, then abruptly took her by the wrist again and replaced the bangle. 'I have just thought of the locket you were wearing. Where is it?'

Diane remembered instantly that it lay on the carpet in the main section of the tent, where he had flung it and where in her tiredness she had forgotten to retrieve it. She clenched her teeth together and gave him a mutinous look.

He studied her, then clicked his fingers together. 'I know where I shall find it! Get dressed for supper, some food inside you might make you less mulish.'

'May I have my supper in here?' she asked.

'No, you will have it with me in the other apartment.' And before she could argue with him the Sheik swept aside the scarlet hanging and left her gazing at the space where he had stood. Still she could see his face and figure and feel the breathtaking vitality about him. She didn't need to be told that never in his life had he allowed a mere girl to defy him ... no doubt as the Caid of the Beni-Haran he had never known a woman who wished to deny him whatever he desired.

Diane fingered the garments he had ordered her to wear. There was a delicate silk slip in a peach colour, pants that were almost transparent, and a kaftan of apricot silk, with a pair of slippers whose toes were tilted.

She had to wear these Eastern things or eat her supper

draped in a towel ... an alternative not even to be
thought about. Biting her lip as even the fine silk hurt
her skin, Diane put on the clothes and then studied her
reflection in a mirror on the chest. With her page-boy
hair and sun-scorched skin she hardly looked a figure of
Eastern delight, which was something to be thankful for.
While she looked so quaint she was hardly in danger of
arousing the Sheik's sensuality, and if her skin started to
peel she would gain a little more safety from his attentions.

Dieu! She caught her breath in a sigh. What a situation! He really meant what he said about sending her
locket to Grandpère and there was no way she could
stop him.

Feeling absurd in the silk kaftan and the tilt-toed slippers, she stood gathering the nerve to enter his presence.
Her hand shook as she forced herself to draw aside the
hanging that partitioned the two sections of the *grande*
tent. He was standing tall at the other entrance, which
was fixed back so the flickering fires could be seen, and
robed figures going about their various tasks. She could
hear music being played, strangely off-key to her ears,
thrumming out there in the firelit night, a combination
of zithers and skin-topped drums. She had heard such
instruments played at the hotel, but the music had lacked
the desert atmosphere of the *douar*.

Diane was intensely aware of being a lone white girl
among a tribe of Arabs; she had nothing with which to
defend herself; the small gun she had been carrying had
been confiscated by the Sheik when he had found her in
the desert. He had probably removed it while she was
barely conscious, before giving her the lemonade which
had revived her with its cool sweetness.

Her hand clenched the scarlet hanging as her gaze

travelled down the long hard length of him as he stood gazing out upon his encampment. He couldn't have stood there with his back to her had the gun still been in her possession. Desperation might have driven her to make use of it. Diane doubted if she had the nerve to kill a man, but a bullet in the leg would have disabled him and kept her safe, at least, from his threat to take her piece by piece.

'Sit down and rest your ankle.' He flung the words over his shoulder. 'It won't mend if you stand on it.'

With his alert hearing he must have caught the sound of her uneven breathing, and giving his back a murderous look Diane hobbled painfully to the ottoman and sat down among the big cushions. He swung round to look at her, and she saw his lips twitch. He ran his gaze from her hair down to her bandaged ankle. 'Settle back and relax,' he said. 'I should have to be feeling desperately amorous if I leapt on you right now.' He came over to her and taking hold of her feet lifted her legs on to the divan. With his lean fingers he felt her ankle, pressing quite gently against the bone. 'Yes, it is a wrench. How did you come to fall off your mount? I would have taken a bet that the granddaughter of Philippe Ronay was able to ride as he was a desert cavalryman.'

'I can ride,' she rejoined. 'A swarm of locusts attacked the oasis at Fetna and my mount took fright and bolted. I'm not used to the Arab type of saddle and he managed to toss me.'

'Locusts at Fetna, eh?' The Sheik regarded her through narrowed eyes. 'Were there a great number of them?'

'A large swarm.' Diane gave a shudder at the memory. 'They covered everything in a matter of seconds, every bush and branch and leaf.'

'Yourself included, eh?' His eyes flicked her hair. 'They

got into your hair and you could feel their legs scraping your skin.'

'One of the beastly things flew down the neck of my shirt,' she confided. 'I—I panicked as much as the horse. They are horrible, aren't they?'

'Yes, and they can strip a field of crops or an orchard of fruit in less than an hour. I think I had better get word to Shemara that they might be heading in that direction. We have a large date plantation there, and we also grow figs and apricots. Making desert land arable is a hard, long task and I wouldn't want such effort to end in the jaws of the locusts. As you say, *bint*, they are a plague. You will excuse me while I go and talk to a lieutenant of mine. I shan't be many minutes away, but if the food should arrive in the meantime then proceed with your own meal. I am sure you are ravenous.'

He strode from the tent, pausing outside to release the flaps so she was concealed. She heard him give an order in Arabic and knew that he had posted a guard at the tent entrance. He knew that her ankle was too painful to be used and she could only surmise that he left someone to guard her in case one of his tribesmen should feel curious enough to take a look at her. Grandpère had once told her that Arabs, especially the high-born ones, were incredibly strict about the privacy of their women and maintained private quarters for them where only members of the family ever set foot.

Diane glanced about her and felt already that she was being kept in seclusion by the Sheik. In *purdah*, didn't they call it? Would he order her to wear a veil like Yasmina?

Her fingers clenched hold of a cushion, arabesqued with silver embroidery and plump with downy feathers. Even in the desert he obviously liked a certain amount of

comfort and luxury. The copper lamps were veined with
a metal which looked like silver, and there were some
items of Oriental furniture in a silvery wood whose carving had a chased look. The effect against the mellow
Bedouin carpets was rich and tasteful in a way Diane
tried to resist. She didn't want to admire anything associated with Khasim ben Haran and told herself it was
all the more reprehensible that a man who spoke two
European languages and liked his surroundings to be im-
peccable should at heart be as uncivilised as desert
tribesmen who never saw the inside of a schoolroom.

She tensed as there was a sudden stirring outside the
tent, then the flap was lifted and Achmed appeared. He
carried a silver tray to the divan table and rested it there.
There were several domed dishes, a gleaming coffee-pot
and a pair of coffee cups in brass holders. The aroma of
the food mingling with the tang of coffee made Diane
feel almost desperately hungry. It had been hours since
she had any food inside her and she couldn't resist the
meal the Sheik provided even though it would have fed
her pride to have refused it.

Achmed met her eyes and indicated with a dark-
skinned hand that she eat and drink. '*Merci*,' she said,
and with a polite inclination of his turbaned head he
withdrew and left her to eat in peace. The coffee was
spicy but nonetheless welcome and right away it made
her feel less fatigued. She served herself with lamb chops
cooked in a gravy flavoured with herbs, dumplings, car-
rots and onions. Food had never tasted so good and she
ate hungrily, spooning up the gravy and the dumplings
that melted in the mouth. She had two of the chops and
cleaned her plate with a slice of tawny bread, which had
a thick delicious crust. The bread was so good that she
spread another slice with creamy cheese and ate this

with a slice of melon. There were some little cakes tasting of honey and stuffed with sultanas and she enjoyed several with some more coffee.

She was eating plump, nutty dates when the Sheik returned, crossing the tent with an agile, almost savage grace of movement. He inspected what remained under the domes of the dishes and quirked a black eyebrow.

'You were hungry indeed, *bint*. It's just as well that I accepted the invitation of Sayed Hamoud to eat supper with him. He has now ridden off to Shemara to warn about the locusts and the Shemaran dates will be already harvested if the locusts should attack. Those dates you are enjoying are from our trees, we also grow our own coffee and most of our crops. We are a self-supporting community in a number of ways.'

'And you are lord of the castle,' she said, feeling each separate nerve grow tense when he sat down on the ottoman beside her and reached for the coffee pot.

'I am the Caid of the *kasbah*.' He sat back to drink his coffee, his eyes flicking her feet from which the *babouches* had slipped to the floor. Diane felt his gaze almost like a touch as it travelled over her slim ankles and along the arches of her feet to her toes, which she thrust into hiding beneath a cushion. 'I'm not one of your stout and idle sheiks, *bint*, who squats among cushions and is waited upon hand and foot. I find great joy in the desert which for me is a place of recreation, timeless and eternal, and also quite excitingly unpredictable, like a lazy animal that might stir at any moment into a raging temper. The desert and the ocean have much in common with each other. A man has to be wary of both of them to survive, but they engender in him a freedom of spirit which is stifled by city life. The desert is in the very souls of the Beni-Haran, its sunlight and storms; its cruelties and pleasures. We are the sons of the stars; the sands are ingrained in our very skins.'

'Yet you appear to like comfort.' Diane gestured around the tent. 'Your carpets are beautiful and your furniture looks as if it must be antique. You don't live like a desert spartan, Sheik Khasim.'

'In a goathair tent like a nomad?' His eyes quizzed her face, a sardonic smile in them. 'I am my people's Caid and I can't live an entirely simple life even if I wished to do so. Don't you find my tent to your liking, even if you find your host—hateful?'

Diane lowered her gaze and licked nervously at her lips, still sweet from the dates. Her fingers were also sticky and she dabbed them in the little bowl of water on the tray. 'As your people's Caid, wouldn't it be polite of you to—to let me leave your *douar* in the morning?'

He sat there silently and when she glanced up at him, she caught her breath at the way his eyes had hardened. 'I have a score to settle with an old enemy, *bint*, and you won't be leaving until it's settled. Like a scorpion it won't cease to sting until the feelings of Philippe Ronay are as butchered as the Beni-Haran were, made to pay for a crime against the colonists which they had not committed. I shall make of his precious granddaughter one of those creatures who sit in their lighted windows, *bint*, and offer for sale all the joys of the damned. What happens to you after you have served your purpose will not concern me.'

Diane, coiled and tensed in every nerve, couldn't take her eyes from his face as he spoke. She watched, fearful and yet fascinated, the flare to his nostrils as he remembered his own youthful terror when his mother died in his arms, his blood mingling with hers as it ran from his cruelly slashed face. Because she was a Ronay she had released in him this cruel need for desert justice ... her breath caught sharply in her throat when he leaned towards her, his hands flexing as if he felt like taking her by the neck and snapping the bone. Her eyes dilated and she could feel her body vibrating to the heavy beat of her heart. Her lips moved in silent appeal and she saw his lips twist into a narrow smile.

'You know, don't you, that I mean every word I say?' His hand reached out and enclosed her undamaged ankle, pulling her foot from beneath the cushion where it was hiding. He stroked his thumb against her instep and let his fingers travel along her foot until their tips were penetrating between her toes.

'Don't do that!' She tried to pull free of his hand, but instantly his fingers locked around her foot and he laughed softly, mockingly.

'Such a small foot, *bint*, and so smooth and sensitive to the touch. The feet of our women grow hard and flat from walking barefoot, but in every possible way you are a girl who has been pampered and guarded—that your indulgent grandparent should allow you to visit the desert without a chaperone is truly amazing.'

'As if he would!' Diane retorted. 'I told you, my chaperone is at Dar-Arisi and will have raised the alarm when I didn't return for lunch at the hotel. You can't keep me here undetected——'

'You think not?' He lifted a taunting eyebrow. 'Do you imagine I would leave to chance the possibility that you have a chaperone at Dar-Arisi? I shall send a man there to find out if you were travelling alone, but I already know the answer. I don't think you like the company of chattering fools and bores, for I don't imagine that Ronay was ever a bore. A man with his experience and past would be a constant source of interest to a young girl

with an enquiring mind; you have often sat at his knee
and listened to his adventures, eh? The great cavalry
hero, with his military medals in a case and his great
scarlet cloak hanging in a cupboard for his granddaughter to admire and perhaps put around her slim
body. How well the scarlet of the cloak and the gold of
your hair would blend together. How romantic to have a
grandpère who rode Arabian horses across the burning
sands, his fierce, hawk-eyed Spahis riding at his spurred
heels, trained to obey his every order.' The Sheik paused
significantly, his eyes holding hers.

'A man with such memories will know what to imagine when the word reaches him, along with the locket
from your neck, that you are somewhere deep in the
desert with a tribesman who has sworn to take an eye
for an eye, a tooth for a tooth . . . a chastity for a murder.'

With each word Diane's skin was flinching as if from
a whip. As physically beaten as she was, she had never
been so accutely aware of another person. She couldn't
drag her gaze from the tawny face; from the arrogant
features and the bone-deep scar. She felt as if she had
been dragged into his eyes to share the cruel memories
that haunted him. His proximity was a menace to every
atom of her womanhood . . . in this respect she had been
kept young by her grandfather, and now she had to face
the fact that she was a woman in the hands of an Arab
whose authority in this region of the desert was absolute.

An Arab, to whom a woman was a creature without a
soul.

'The bones in your foot,' he murmured, 'are like those
in a quail.'

She felt her foot jump nervously as if he prodded it
with a pin. A naked entreaty sprang into her eyes.

'Haven't you any mercy in you?' she asked. 'Are you really such a—brute?'

'The emotion that I feel is brutal. It has to be slaked and then I shall be free of it. Seeing you here like this convinces me that destiny weaves the pattern we must follow.'

'Your people know I'm here—they'll expect you to return me to my people.' She tried to speak convincingly, but her voice faltered when he smiled as if at a fool.

'The obligations of my rank do not include my private behaviour with a woman—if you comprehend my meaning?'

All too vividly did Diane comprehend the meaning implicit in the look the Sheik swept over her, making her aware as never before in her life that she was alone with a man to whom a female was a source of recreation, akin to hawking in the desert or hunting for gazelle.

He sat there beside her in all his brazen strength, and she saw the hunting light in his eyes ... eyes that in their dominance held her as a hawk holds the pigeon it swoops upon with savage intent.

It was all there, stamped into his features as he lounged against the cushions. This man would force her into his arms and he wouldn't release her until it suited him to do so. Education and ethics had nothing to do with this side to him ... the scar he carried had bitten deep into his soul, and because he was an Arab he believed in *mektub*, in the strange workings of fate that had drawn her to the desert.

For a long time Diane had felt the attraction of the East working upon her imagination and hopelessly she had to admit that nothing would have kept her from coming here. Nor would all the wishing in the world whisk her away from this encampment on a magic carpet.

Softly, at perfect melodic pitch, the Sheik began to whistle, reminding her of the way he had whistled his hawk to him in the desert. Diane listened and recognised the melody as *Chanson d'un Coeur Brisé*.

Song of a broken heart!

'You—you get unutterable pleasure out of this, don't you?' Her eyes darkened with torment as she looked at him.

'Of course.' He gave a laugh on the edge of cruelty. 'By Allah, how I've waited for this hour! I little dreamed that it would come in the shape of a girl, but we say in the East that debts are paid not in the same coin but in unexpected ways.'

'Cruel ways,' she breathed. 'In keeping with what you are!'

'What am I, woman?' He slid a hand along the divan until it was only a fraction of an inch from her silk-clad hip. 'I know what you are, but I plead curiosity about your knowledge of men—I think you have had little to do with them apart from your noble grandfather, so how would you presume to judge me?'

'As I've said before, Sheik Khasim, one look is sufficient to tell me that you're an autocrat who bends the rules to suit yourself.'

'I could certainly bend you without any effort,' he agreed, a smile curling about his lips as he slid his hand on to her hip and gripped the bone as she tensed and then shuddered. 'What delight there is in touching a woman, every bone and curve and inch of skin is to the masculine hand a delicate work of art he knows he could crush in his fingers. I could break you apart, *bint*, and scatter the pieces down some disused well in the depths of the desert. I could be that sort of man for all you know.'

'No,' she shook her head and felt his touch seeping warm through the silk where his fingers gripped her, not bruisingly but almost caressingly, his eyes watching her face as he moved his fingertips against her body. 'You're more subtle than that, Sheik Khasim. I know how your mind is working—you want to send me back to my grandfather with my spirit broken, not my body.'

'Clever girl,' he murmured. 'And one hears tales of golden-haired women being rather obtuse.'

'I can hardly believe that I'm the first fair-haired woman you've had in your tent.' Diane tried to disengage her mind from her body so she wouldn't feel his hand as it travelled up her leg and fondled her through the soft silk. Tiny, deep-seated nerves convulsed at his touch and tormentedly she smacked away his hand, glaring at him as he laughed at her, the pupils of her eyes enormously dark against the blue irises.

'By Allah, those eyes of yours would be worth a fortune strung on gold.' The laugh died away in the depths of his throat. 'How fortunate for me that fate and Philippe Ronay made you the way you are, Diane. Already you are beginning to look less sun-broiled and in a day or two I shall quite look forward to coming home to my tent to find you waiting for me.'

His words sank like knives into Diane's mind ... waiting here in this tent, dreading the moment when he would take possession of her, unlovingly, driven by his need to assuage the anguish of what cold steel had done to the Beni-Haran in the burning sunlight of the desert.

She had to pay the price ... the demand was there in the Sheik's dark and pitiless eyes.

CHAPTER THREE

'I SHALL be waiting for you with a knife if I get my hands on one!' Diane didn't care that the words sounded like a line from a melodrama ... she meant them.

'It runs in your blood,' he drawled. 'We are what we learn and inherit from those who breed us. You're a Ronay and thrusting a knife into me is bred in your bones, lovely though they are under that silky white skin. It is written, Diane. You and I were meant to cross blades from the moment we opened our eyes, you in a nursery of flounced chintz, no doubt, me under the desert stars upon a rug on the sands. My mother was travelling in the desert with my father when my time came to be born, so I'm truly a son of the sands. The first breath I took was of desert air and I shall die here when the time comes—though I intend to make sure that knives are never left within reach of your hand.'

'Don't be too sure of yourself.' Diane braved his eyes even as the nerves cringed inside her at the ruthless grace and strength of him beside her, his deep scar cleft with shadow where the lamplight failed to reach. 'When you aren't here at the encampment how are you going to stop me from running away? Are you going to hobble me, like a goat tied up for nightfall and the tiger?'

'It's an amusing thought.' A smile strayed in and out of his eyes. 'My little scapegoat, eh? Our favourite endearment for a woman is gazelle.'

'I wouldn't want your endearments if they came gift-wrapped!' she retorted. 'Are you absolutely certain that there isn't anyone in this camp who might like it to be known that you're holding a European woman against her will?'

'It wouldn't occur to my people, Diane, that you are here in my tent as an unwilling guest.'

'God, you're arrogant!' she gasped. 'Your people know I'm a stranger you found exhausted in the desert——'

'We are Arabs and it's our custom to offer shelter and hospitality to a stranger in need of it. That's exactly what I'm doing, am I not? I have seen to it that you have been bathed, clothed and fed.'

'A guest isn't refused the right to leave if she so wishes.'

'Ah, but as you have sampled my hospitality it will look as if you don't wish to leave, and as I'm the Caid of the Beni-Haran no one will bother to come and ask if it's true or false. You remain my guest whether you like it or not.'

Diane stared at him, stricken into silence and terribly aware that in this region of the desert his word was law and a woman his for the taking if he so wished it.

She helplessly realised that to the Sheik's people she was no more than a ripe fruit he desired ... she saw the mockery glinting in his eyes as he reached for a fig from the fruit dish and casually stripped the leaf before biting into it.

'What I do with you, *bint*, will not concern my tribesmen. Their women might be curious and wonder what I see in a girl with slightly turned hips and hair cut close to the nape. The hair will soon start to grow, for I would prefer you to look less like a pretty boy.'

'I've no intention of staying here until my hair grows long enough to satisfy you.' Even to Diane her tone of voice sounded more defiant than confident. 'You won't find me as compliant as the women of your harem. They might fall at your feet, but I shan't!'

'I have only to touch you and you tremble,' he mocked, and again with slow deliberation he ran his hand along her silk-trousered leg. She watched his hand as if mesmerised, noticing how darkly tanned the skin was against the pastel silk.

'Don't scream,' he smiled teasingly, 'the time for play is not yet. When your skin is back to normal and doesn't smart at the merest touch, then shall I teach you to be a woman. We are all creatures of sensuality when the mood is right, as you will learn, *chérie*.'

'Don't you dare call me that!' Driven by fear and temper, she struck at him and landed a blow against his scar. He didn't appear to feel anything, but she had felt the jagged edges against her fingers. 'Oh, don't you realise—my grandfather is well known in France and I can't just vanish without the authorities being notified. When they find me you'll be jailed!'

'And what a scandal will result when all the gaudy details are printed in the daily papers! Can't you just imagine the avid interest in reading about Colonel Ronay's granddaughter being kept a prisoner of pleasure by a desert chief?' The Sheik smiled and blew on his fingertips. 'The sensation-seekers will love it and lap up every torrid phrase, and how the proud head of Philippe Ronay will sink low when he has to sit in court and hear you give evidence against me. I shall plead my crime as one of passion and produce witnesses to prove Colonel Ronay's crime against the Beni-Haran. In this very encampment there are people who remember that day as clearly as I do and if they knew right now that I have in my tent the granddaughter of that accursed man, they would demand that I return you to where I found you and leave you to perish in the teeth of a wild animal. Shall I do it, *bint*? It will certainly save your honoured grandfather from public exposure, will it not?'

Diane stared at the proud hard face of Khasim ben Haran and she could hardly bear it that he should speak so harshly about her grandfather, who had always been loving and kindly towards her, teaching her about books and art as well as sharing with her the battle tactics of the model soldiers on the great oak table in his den. She had to judge him as she knew him, and loved him.

'You cruel swine,' she said distinctly to the Sheik. 'You judge everyone by your own arrogant nature—I'd sooner take my chance in the desert than have to endure your company. You're the animal!'

Silence struck through the tent and Diane watched as the sabre cut stood out lividly against the tawny skin of the Sheik's face. She knew that no one had ever flung such an insult in his face and she was glad to have done it ... if to his own people he was high and mighty, to her he was just a desert barbarian.

She braced herself against his retaliation, feeling the nerves vibrate under her skin when he surged to his feet with an agile panther movement.

'Speak to me again like that,' he said through his teeth, 'and I shall sell you into one of the lowest pleasure houses in Algiers where, my lady, your proud spirit will soon be humbled. There you will lie in the arms of the unwashed and submit your lips to the reeking mouths of drug addicts and creatures who are less than animals. Don't fool yourself that I would hesitate because you are young and innocent.' He paused there and gave her an intent look. 'I want the pleasure of breaking your Ronay spirit myself.'

'And what do you intend to use?' she asked scornfully. 'Spurs and a whip?'

'No, *bint*,' he leaned down to her and she saw deep in his eyes a derisive glint, 'I have at my disposal far more subtle tools than those I use on my horses.'

His meaning sank into her mind, invading her senses as she noticed the smooth hardness of his chest in the opening of his dark silk kaftan, the play of the muscles beneath his brown skin. She was a girl who had known only the company of an elderly grandparent for nine years; she had been cloistered against the potency of younger men, least of all the smouldering sensual force she could feel in this Sheik of the desert.

Defensively she drew away from him. Her throat had gone almost as dry as when she had lain in the desert at the mercy of the sun. He slowly straightened to his full height, the lamplight slanting on to his sable hair, his left profile turned away from her.

'The hour grows late,' he said, 'and your stress must be relieved by sleep. Come, let me assist you to the bed.' He extended a hand, but Diane refused to accept it. There was only one bed in the sleeping area of the tent and weary as she felt she didn't intend to share it with him.

'I—I shall be all right here,' she said. 'This divan is big enough for me and there are plenty of cushions——'

'Little fool,' impatiently he reached for her and swung her up into his arms, striding brusquely with her into the other room. 'You need rest if you are to regain your looks. Right now I find you as unappealing as a boiled prawn.'

He placed her on the bed and indicated the sleeping robe at the foot of it. 'You will find that a little large, but I advise you to wear it. We are in the desert and there are all kinds of *bêtes noires* that fly and creep in the night. Can you manage alone or shall I send a woman to assist you?'

Diane shook her head. 'I shall be all right—I wonder, though, if I could have a glass of lemonade? I still feel rather dry.'

'I shall order it.' He glanced intently around the sleeping area, taking the lamp from the bedside table and playing its light into the corners of the room. Diane swallowed nervously and knew he was looking for the *bêtes noires* that crept and crawled in the night. Satisfied, he replaced the lamp on the table, then gave her one of his encompassing looks. His eyes were so riveting that she couldn't avoid them, nor could she avoid noticing how the bed-lamp threw the shadows of his dark lashes on to the planes of his face. She couldn't help but wonder how many other women had lain on this bed and gazed upwards into those compelling Arabian eyes ... women who had no doubt welcomed him into their arms, their lips only too eager to meet the passion and tenacity that shaped his mouth.

All that was virginal and untried in Diane shrank away from all that was masculine and certain in Khasim ben Haran. He saw this and his eyes glinted with devilry.

'In your present state you have no need to fear my advances,' he drawled. 'I don't number among my vices the tormenting of tired, sunburned, frightened virgins.'

'Don't you?' she said huskily. 'What do you think you've been doing ever since you brought me to your encampment? What do you think I feel, knowing what it will do to my grandfather when he receives my locket a-and those lies you intend him to believe?'

'That you are in the hands of some scavenger of the sands?' The firm lips twisted and the dark eyes hardened. 'My heart bleeds for him!'

'Oh, you're so cruel——' Diane turned her head away from the Sheik and her lips were trembling. 'Wouldn't it be enough, if you did—did what you have to do to me, but left him alone?'

'A noble sacrifice, *bint*, but it just wouldn't suffice. We Arabs are a subtle people and it will be a refinement of justice for Ronay to imagine his pure young grand-daughter being slowly degraded. For each Beni-Haran life his men took that day, his granddaughter will spend a night in arms he will envisage as lustful as they are layered by grime. He will imagine you locked in an em-brace so awful he will spend his nights pacing the floor of hell. He will hear your piteous cries—a tear for every tear a Beni-Haran woman wept over the body of a hus-band or a child. He will have you back when I have finished with you!'

The Sheik turned away from the bed and swept open the scarlet hanging. 'Your lemonade will be brought to you. Sleep well!'

'Go to hell yourself, you son of Shaitan!' Diane replied, knowing this to be extremely insulting to an Arab. But all he did was to laugh low in his throat, as if her bite was no more than that of a midge he carelessly brushed away from him.

Diane crouched for long moments on the bed without moving, then she caught the aroma of *cigarro* smoke in her nostrils and envisaged the Sheik loungingly at ease on the divan in the other portion of the tent, careless of her feelings and pleased that fate had supplied him with the means to avenge his mother.

She clutched her arms around herself and knew he would be quite merciless about it, and unless she found some means of escape from the *douar* the night would soon come when instead of the jingle of an ankle bracelet as Yasmina brought lemonade to the bedside, the Sheik himself would join her.

'The *sitt* looks very weary——'

'Yasmina,' Diane caught desperately at the Arabian girl's wrist, 'you look kind a-and I need help so badly. I have to get away from this place—will you help me? Will you—please!'

Yasmina gazed down at Diane and a look of sympathy came into her brown eyes. '*Sitt*, I dare not oppose my lord Khasim in any way. He will himself take you back to where you belong——'

'He won't!' Diane shook her head almost frenziedly. 'He means to keep me here against my will—I don't want to stay with him, but he refuses to let me return to my family. I—I must have someone's help—if you could get me a horse, I could ride away and he'd never know that you aided me.'

'He would know, *sitt*.' Yasmina shook a regretful head. 'The Sheik is all-seeing, very shrewd and powerful, as he must be to rule the Beni-Haran. My own brother would take a whip to me if I did anything to oppose the Sheik's wishes——'

'Whip you?' Diane looked appalled. 'Your own brother?'

Yasmina spread her hands speakingly. 'If my lord Khasim has a desire to keep you with him, *lel-lah*, then he must have his reason. If his glance has fallen upon you with favour, then you should feel honoured.'

'Honoured?' Outrage filled Diane's eyes. 'I want none of him, don't you understand? All I want is to get away from him as far as possible! You're a woman, Yasmina, so you must understand how I feel. If you were held captive by a man you dislike would you tamely submit to him?'

'I am Arabian, *sitt*. My brother is my guardian and he may one day wish me to marry a man I have never seen.'

'But that's too barbarous!' Diane looked shocked. 'It's turn of the century that Arabian men should have such power over women! Haven't you desert people moved with the times?'

'Our laws and our ways suit us,' Yasmina murmured. 'That is why many of us still wear the veil. The Sidi Khasim doesn't insist upon it for the women of the Beni-Haran, but our own fathers and brothers prefer that our features should be covered in case they incite lust in a man. You see how it is with yourself, *sitt*.'

'You think I've incited lust in your Sheik in this state?' Diane swept a hand down her person and her laugh was ragged. 'If I told you my name was Ronay would that explain better why he won't let me go?'

'Ronay?' Yasmina's eyes widened as she studied Diane, and then she backed away from the bed.

'You see,' Diane almost whispered, 'now you don't like me.'

'My parents were killed in that raid,' Yasmina said quietly. 'My brother Sayed was minding the sheep in the hills and he took me with him that day. When we came home to camp——' Yasmina lowered her gaze from Diane's face. 'It is better that you don't tell anyone else, *sitt*. Now shall I help you to undress for bed?'

By now Diane was feeling weak as a kitten and she tiredly acquiesced. Yasmina's hands were as gentle as ever, but she no longer had much to say and Diane realised that she had been unwise to tell the girl her name. If there had been the remotest hope that Yasmina would help her, it had now vanished. Yasmina and her brother were caught up in the Sheik's revenge and whatever he decreed for Philippe Ronay's granddaughter would find favour with them. They too were part of the desert law that said that an eye should be plucked if an eye was taken.

Wearing the bed robe, in which she could wrap her feet, Diane slid beneath the covers of the bed. The beautiful silk cover was removed and folded and a large sheepskin replaced it.

'The nights grow cold,' Yasmin explained, handing Diane her glass of lemonade. The glass, like the coffee cups, was in a delicately filigreed holder, and when Diane sipped the lemonade she found that it had a subtly different flavour.

'Is there something in this?' she asked, and even as her pulses jolted she dismissed the notion that the Sheik would drug her in order to have his way with her. It was hardly his line to give a girl knockout drops; he wanted the fun and fury of taming her to his hand when she was fully aware of him.

'The merest addition of something that will make the *sitt* sleep deeply, so that in the morning the effects of the sunburn will not be quite so painful. It doesn't make the drink taste unpleasant?'

'No, quite the reverse.' Reassured Diane finished the lemonade and handed the glass to Yasmina. Already she could feel a lethargy stealing over her and she surrendered her tired aching body to the downy softness of the pillows and drew the sheepskin close against her. Sleep would stifle for a while the tormenting thoughts that buzzed about in her mind like so many gnats with a sharp bite. In the morning she would feel stronger and more able to cope with the situation in which she found herself. In an Arab camp there were plenty of horses and when she could get hold of one she'd be off like the wind. The Sheik seemed to take it for granted she was an inept horsewoman, but her grandfather had had her taught riding by his batman, one of the best cavalrymen until an unlucky bullet had injured his spine and made him unfit for the long desert gallops undertaken by the Spahis. Diane had been at home with horses since a child and she was totally fearless in the saddle. It was Coco, her grandfather's batman, who had taught her certain words to which Arabian horses responded. They might, with any luck, be her password out of the *douar* of Khasim ben Haran.

She snuggled down into the deeply comfortable bed and the thought drifted across her mind that he would have a responsive couch in which to woo his doe-eyed conquests. Here, no doubt, a honey-skinned chain of them had passed through his lean dark hands; here on these very pillows raven hair had spread like rich silk, cushioning some pretty, full-lipped face as he ran those hands down over smooth shoulders to the quivering arch of hips that were seductively rounded.

Diane closed her eyes against the turbulence of her thoughts ... such images had never entered her head until now ... until tonight she had slept in a single bed in a chaste white room in a Breton house; a room as far removed from barbaric splendour as she was from the beloved old house that overlooked the sea, with its high-pitched roof and narrow gothic tower in which her room right now was silent and shadowed, her well-thumbed books and other belongings out of reach.

Diane felt a clutch of panic in case she should never see them again, especially the worn, sun-weathered face of her grandfather.

'Would you like me to turn out the lamp?' Yasmina asked.

'Please.' In the darkness she wouldn't see the trappings of the tent, so disturbing and strange.

'*Leyltak sayeedah, sitt.*' The lamp went out and left a tang of cassia oil in the air. The partition fell into place behind the quiet figure of Yasmina and as Diane closed her heavy eyes the drifting smoke of a *cigarro* was a tormenting reminder that she was a prisoner in the Sheik's camp. Kismet, he had called it, that she of all people should fall into his hands, and lying here on the edge of sleep she remembered what Coco had said to her the day before she departed from Brittany:

'It's the call of the sands, *mademoiselle*. You have to go and find out why they call you.'

Diane slept for hours, warm as a beaver in the sheepskin. The outline of her slender body was barely visible in the deep wide bed and she slept so soundly that she was unaware that someone came more than once to the bedside, bending over her to hold a hand near her lips in order to feel her breath. A deep voice murmured words she wouldn't have understood; a few more hours passed and though daylight came into the tent, Diane slept on undisturbed.

She awoke of her own accord, rising up out of the depths of sleep to a feeling of refreshment, followed by the pangs of hunger and a need to visit the bathroom.

The covers slipped from her shoulders as she sat up and ran dazed eyes around the tent. She had to be dreaming, and then as full comprehension returned to her a pang of another sort was added to those she was already feeling. Her gaze settled on a painted screen in a corner of the sleeping area and swinging her legs out of bed she hastened across the carpeted floor to the screen. To her relief she discovered a commode, its bowl shiningly clean beneath the wooden lid. Diane took grateful advantage of the commode, aware that encamped Arabs made use of the sand itself. She also found that a bowl of water had been placed on a table for her use, along with a sponge, a bar of sandalwood soap and a big, soft-textured towel. She removed the enveloping robe and examined her legs and arms. They looked less painfully red, but some of the skin was already peeling from her neck and her nose and her skin smarted when she applied the soap. After washing she looked around in the hope of finding her own breeches and shirt, but instead a cotton tunic-like dress had been left in readiness for her, and some underthings that could only be referred to as bloomers and a petticoat. She put them on and felt as if she had stepped out of the pages of *Little Women*. It seemed all too obvious that desert people didn't keep up with the times!

Dressed and feeling a lot less sun-sore, Diane went to the dressing-table and tidied her hair with a tortoiseshell comb which matched the initialled brush. She touched the letter K with a fingertip, and the next instant felt her entire body going taut as in the mirror she saw the scarlet hanging moved aside in order to provide entrance for a tall figure clad in a white tunic open at the neck and bound around the body by an embossed leather belt. The breeches beneath the tunic were latched into riding boots that fitted close against the strong legs. The entire man looked powerful and vigorous and he seemed to bring with him a dash of desert air.

'Ah, you are awake and dressed!' Through the mirror the shock of his dark eyes was penetrating, sliding down over her figure in the rather shapeless dress. 'How are you feeling after such a profound sleep?'

'A lot better, thank you.' Diane laid down the comb

and turned around to face him; she felt very conscious of her peeling nose and the way the dress hung upon her like a sack. She expected him to laugh mockingly, but instead he came to her and took hold of her wrist, watching her face as he checked her pulse.

He nodded. 'You haven't developed sun-fever, which is something of a miracle as you lay in the sun for some time.' Abruptly he touched her hair, pushing his fingers into its Greuze-gold thickness. Though trimmed into her nape her hair had an almost pelt-like quality, heavy and not easy to manage when allowed to grow long in the way her grandfather preferred; when Diane wore it long she twisted it into a snake's tail and pinned it at her nape.

Right now she could feel hard fingertips against her neck and she wanted to twist out of the Sheik's grasp, but sensed that it was wiser to remain quiescent.

'The *malaise* of yesterday has left you, eh?' He tilted her head so she had to meet his eyes, which scanned every inch of her face and settled on her mouth. 'Yes, *bint*, your looks begin to recover, but I would advise that you continue for a while to grease your skin; you don't wish to scar its fine whiteness in any way, do you?'

At his mention of that word her gaze was drawn to his own scar; he would have been about thirteen when it happened, she realised, and a boy of that age was old enough to remember the pain and emotional agony of what had occurred. In a way she could understand his bitterness, but it didn't justify his intentions with regard to her. Diane tightened her lips. She wouldn't waste breath pleading with him but would await her chance to steal a horse.

'I—I hope I'm not to be kept in this tent like a prisoner?' she said. 'I need some air and I want to stretch my legs.'

'No doubt in the direction of Dar-Arisi,' he drawled. 'The next time you venture alone into the desert, Diane, you might not be so fortunate as to be found and cared for.'

His casual use of her name inflamed Diane, and yet at the same time she knew she could do nothing to stop him. For now he had the advantage over her and a slight show of submission might get her what she wanted in the long run.

'Come, we will eat lunch.' His fingers gripped her elbow and she gave him a startled glance. They entered the larger portion of the tent and proceeded outside to where a camp table was laid beneath the stretched awning on poles. Achmed was busy beside a camp fire, where a long-spouted coffee pot was standing on hot ashes.

'You have slept away the morning,' the Sheik told Diane, as he drew out one of the canvas chairs from the table, 'but I can see from your astonished look that it isn't a regular indulgence.'

'No indeed.' She sat down in the chair and was intensely aware of the Sheik standing over her before he took his place at the opposite side of the table. In order to avoid his eyes, and also because she was curious, Diane let her gaze travel around the encampment. She saw at once that it was above the level of the desert and set out on a hillside that caught what cooling breezes there were. She saw beyond the scattering of black tents some herds of grazing animals, among them a number of sleek horses, and hope lit up inside her that she might manage to get hold of one. Arab horses were fleet and anywhere out of range of Khasim ben Haran would suit her.

She watched some Beni-Haran women tending the pots on their fires and noticed that like Yasmina some of them were veiled. Dark veils that gave them a mysterious look, with a glint of gold jewellery against their sombre robes. She sensed that they were watching her, though the tribesmen who passed by, always with a *salaam* to the Sheik, barely gave her a glance. It was considered impolite, she knew, for Arabs to stare at a woman who belonged to another man. Such a stare might cause hot words and even a show of knives. Her grandfather had told her that though Arabian men did speak of women as creatures who had no souls, they had in reverse a jealous possessiveness towards their bodies.

A tremor of sensual awareness ran through her and she found her gaze drawn back to the Sheik as if he magnetised her. He was watching her through lazily narrowed eyes, a boundless air of authority and masculine assurance about him. Her heart skipped a beat ... there was also a barbarous attraction about him that made him as fascinating to watch as the tawny sands that stretched away from every side of the *douar*. He was part of the desert; his skin held its shadings and his eyes all the menace and danger that lurked in it.

Achmed came to the table with the dishes of food, pot-roasted meat and vegetables in a gravy that made Diane almost groan with hunger. It had to be the desert air that caused such hunger; she just couldn't resist tucking into the meal as if she were ravenous, half-closing her eyes at the deliciousness of the crisply roasted potatoes. At least where food was concerned the Sheik was civilised.

'As the cat closes her eyes in submission to the hand providing the cream,' he murmured.

Diane heard him but refused to look at him. 'Achmed is an excellent cook,' she replied. 'Your camp is a very picturesque one, Sheik Khasim, and I'd quite enjoy being here but for you.'

'Scratch me, *bint*, but you'll find that an Arab's skin is as tough as leather. That is one of the reasons why some of the men like their women to wear the *bui bui*, in case our hot sun should toughen their skins. The veil has a certain seductive quality, has it not?'

'If you mean that it makes women look submissive, yes,' Diane agreed, her glance skimming past his face to watch a woman who was playing nearby with a child, the jewel in her nostril glinting through the fine dark silk of the veil that was draped half across her face. The eyes above the veil met Diane's and there was a certain animosity in her look, and something of scorn as she flicked her eyes over Diane's short shining hair.

'Your people obviously don't find me quite so seductive,' Diane said dryly, amused herself by the child in baggy pants showing his plump belly.

'Don't let it upset you,' the Sheik drawled. 'It isn't my intention that you should wear by day the garments that were provided for when we are alone in my tent. Eastern silk is hand-loomed and there is nothing finer than the soft gleam of it against a woman's skin, especially when that skin is like a pearl washed in milk.'

Diane caught her breath and hastily concealed the sound behind her table napkin. She saw a smile on the edge of his lips, and then he turned to Achmed to indicate that he remove their plates. A dessert of honey pancakes was served to Diane while the Sheik himself had cheese and crisp biscuits with his coffee.

'Our communal life here in the desert is of necessity less than private,' he informed Diane. 'Quite naturally within the next few days my people will assume that I have taken you for my woman. They believe you to be

British. Your colouring assists the deception—it wouldn't do for them to know that you are the granddaughter of the Franzawi colonel many of them have good reason to remember. Only one other shares that secret and I trust him with my life.'

'Not the brother of Yasmina?' Diane asked curiously. 'She told me——'

'What indiscreet remark, *bint*, has passed between the two of you?'

'I mentioned my name to Yasmina and she said her parents died in that raid and her brother was unforgiving about it.'

'As well he might be! No, Sayed is not that far in my confidence, not as yet. Another has ridden to Dar-Arisi to find out if you were travelling alone or with a chaperone. He will be discreet in his enquiries—he is what you call in France my *aide-de-camp*; his loyalty to the Beni-Haran is as firm as my own. In due course he will become the husband of my sister, so he has reason to protect some of our family secrets.'

'You have a sister?' Diane exclaimed.

'Yes.' A black eyebrow took an arrogant tilt. 'Did you imagine that I was conjured out of fire and stone like a demon?'

'It wouldn't surprise me.'

'Of course not,' he mocked. 'My sister is called Morgana and she lives in the *kasbah* at Shemara. You will meet her.'

'I shall do nothing of the sort,' Diane protested, the prongs of her fork jabbing a piece of pancake, as his words had jabbed her. 'It's bad enough that you force me to stay here, but I—I won't be abducted to your house!'

'My *kasbah*,' he corrected her. 'Within its many miles of walls live the people of Shemara, and outside its walls are the plantations. There are dwellings and bazaars rambling beneath its battlements, and windows and balconies are suspended at one side above the sea. For centuries it has guarded the Beni-Haran from pirates on the one hand, and desert intruders on the other. One of its courtyards has seven fountains set within it and the apartments there are those of the women.'

'Your harem,' Diane broke in, colour high on her cheekbones.

'My harem,' he agreed, and his hand was steady as stone as he poured some more of the darkly rich coffee into her cup. 'Does it intrigue your female curiosity, Diane, that I might have other women beside yourself? Did you hope that you were the only rose in my garden?'

'I—I'd like to see you in hell!' Diane flung at him.

'It is well that we converse in English, otherwise such a remark from a woman would warrant a good shaking. As we say, shake your woman as your sheepskin and keep it in order.'

'You people have some charming philosophies with regard to women, haven't you?'

'If you mean that we like to be the master and not the servant, then you are right. As there is honey and gall in most flowers, so there is temper as well as tenderness in women and if the one is allowed to overwhelm the other, then much that is pleasant in life becomes instead a bitter taste in the mouth. A woman's voice was made to speak softly, just as the dove was made to coo on the fountain's rim. Woman was made to melt, not to be hard and resistant. The silken skin and hair which nature gave to her are meant to reflect her inner self, as the pool reflects the palm tree.'

'The palm tree being symbolic of the man, I suppose?'

'You live and learn, *bint*.' He leaned back in his canvas

chair and even as he placed one of his long thin *cigarros* between his lips Achmed was at his side with a flaring match to light it. Diane noticed that he thanked his man-servant and didn't just accept the service as his due. She had to admit to herself that he had courteous manners, but she knew in her deepest instincts that just as the sun overlay the sands so did suavity hide the real Sheik.

No man who dominated a great tribe of desert people could be other than strong-willed, and as feared as he was respected. Arabs didn't look up to a man who was easy-going. The Sheik had to be a law unto himself, and Diane could see the dominance and power in his sun-bronzed features, just as she could see a blend of passion and irony in the shape of his mouth.

She felt sure he enjoyed his harem of women, but she doubted if he loved any of them.

'Much of our art and writing is based on symbols,' he said. 'A great deal of our architecture reflects the feminine outlines of women, her curves and ovals lead-ing into secret places. The male is represented by the hard thrust of the minarets into the vault of heaven.' The Sheik's eyes dwelt intently on Diane's face as if curious to see if she fully understood him. She did, and it took an effort not to glance away from him in a wild sort of shy-ness. She knew he was trying to confuse her for his own amusement; that he meant to wring from her every kind of diversion.

'European buildings have hard outlines,' he said thoughtfully, 'as if the men of those countries are re-luctant to enjoy the feminine shape except in the music halls. Our Eastern attitude to women strikes me as being far more complimentary—as a jewel looks more worth-while in a gold setting so does a woman look best in a fetching garment.'

'Like the women in your harem?' Diane couldn't resist asking.

'You seem very intrigued by my harem.' Aromatic smoke wreathed about his dark eyes and lost itself in his scar. 'Can't you wait to be installed at the court of the seven fountains?'

'You'd have to kill me first,' she retorted.

'That would surely defeat my purpose, Diane.'

'I'm well aware of that, Sheik Khasim.'

'There are European women who long to penetrate the secrets of the Eastern harem,' he said lazily.

'No doubt women who read lurid fiction in which a handsome sheik falls in love with some silly female who swoons all over the cushions and carpets.' Diane gave him a scornful look, though behind it she was quailing in a way she didn't like. This moment and the man facing her were all too real and weren't figments of a writer's imagination. 'I—I can just imagine what the real thing is like!' she added defiantly.

'Can you indeed, *bint*?' His eyes held her gaze and she found herself unable to evade their dark magnetism. She could feel his dominance even though he didn't touch her ... she felt like a hare crouching in the shadow of a sand leopard.

'I'm curious about what you imagine.' Smoke slipped almost insolently from his lips. 'Won't you tell me, then I shall know how you expect to be treated when we're alone.'

'You know better than I do how you treat your women,' she said, and was alarmed at how breathless she felt. 'As if they're slaves—flung aside when you've had enough of them!'

'Is that why you came to the desert, Diane, because somewhere in your cloistered young body there lurked

a longing to be enslaved by someone like me? Did the
environs of your grandfather's house grow tedious when
you grew into a woman and did you imagine a more
exciting desert than the one described to you by a soldier
more accustomed to the barracks and the stable than the
jasmine courts of Arabia?'

'I most certainly didn't visit the desert with the idea
of being abducted by someone like you!' Diane's eyes
blazed into his, and she could feel her hands itching for
the satisfaction of pummelling his arrogant face and the
looming strength of his shoulders. 'How dare you suggest
such a thing?'

'I suggest it, Diane, because we human beings aren't
always aware of the inmost workings of our minds and
hearts. Perhaps you answered a call which was heard
only by your most primitive instincts.'

Diane gave a little shiver and remembered what Coco
had said to her about the call of the sands. Yet, looking
into the Arabian eyes of the Sheik, she had to deny that
such a thing was possible.

'My grandfather spoke so often of the desert that I
grew curious about the place,' she said. 'I wanted to see
Fetna and the fortress where he was stationed—he would
have travelled with me had he been fit enough. I—I appeal to you again, Sheik Khasim. It could come as a bad
shock to him if he's told that I've been abducted—do you
want to be his murderer?'

'In view of what I've told you, *bint*, you should know
the answer to that question.' The Sheik looked and spoke
unrelentingly. 'He had no mercy when he let his Spahis
loose on my people. He had to be aware that it was a
peaceful encampment, but he wanted reprisals and to his
sort all Arabs look alike. The Beni-Haran had nothing to
do with the killing of the French colonials at Abbis-Aba,

but so long as the sands were stained with Arab blood it didn't matter to him that it was the blood of innocent men, women and children. Fifty-six of my people died that day, including my mother, and so will as many days and nights pass, Mademoiselle Ronay, before you are returned to that man's bosom. He will know what it feels like to mourn for someone lost——'

At that point the Sheik abruptly ceased to speak as a woman's scream rang out close by. He was upon his feet instantly and Diane saw that the woman who screamed was the one in the veil who had been playing with her child. The child was now red in the face and appeared to be choking, and when the Sheik reached the little boy he took firm hold of him, up-ended his jerking body and gave him several vigorous shakes. The child spluttered, coughed and out came the date stone which had lodged in his throat. The Sheik righted him, stroked his hair and handed him to his mother, giving her at the same time a smile of such riveting charm that Diane couldn't take her eyes from him. The woman clutched the child to her, and then turning in Diane's direction she pointed a hand at her and broke into a spate of words. The smile was wiped from the Sheik's face and he suppressed the woman's speech by pressing a hand over her veiled mouth. He frowned and spoke firmly to her, while Diane watched the scene and wondered what had made the woman speak so accusingly.

She tensed as he strode back to the table, while the woman and her child withdrew into one of the nearby tents. Khasim ben Haran spread his hands in a very Eastern gesture as he stood over Diane: 'W-what did she say about me?' Diane gazed up at him, still shaken by how near the child had come to choking on the fruit stone.

'She said you had been watching her child with your blue eyes and they had caused him to swallow the stone.'

'Oh no!' Diane pressed a hand to her own throat. 'What a dreadful thing to say!'

'Desert people are superstitious.' He shrugged slightly, as if despite his own education he had to accept that many of his people remained firm in their strange dated beliefs. 'Blue eyes are connected with witchery and your eyes, *bint*, are as intensely blue as sapphires when the sun catches in them. Incredible, really.'

Diane stared up at him; no one in her life had ever implied that her eyes were jewel-coloured, nor had anyone ever connected them with witchery. 'How absurd——'

'That I liken your eyes to sapphires, *bint*?'

'No——' She shook her head. 'That the woman could believe I caused the accident because I admired the child.'

'You are strange to her and she needed to vent her nervous reaction to the incident. In a while you will seem less alien with your gold skin and hair, and your blue eyes.' His teeth showed white against his own bronzed skin. 'Love for a man will soften them to blue satin.'

Her heart lurched and she could hardly believe she had heard him correctly. Oh no, that would be the worst indignity, and yet she had heard of it happening. Abducted women had been known to fall in love with the man who committed the outrage, as if there was a deep primitive urge in a woman to be dragged by her hair into an experience which defied all the conventions.

But Diane didn't want to believe it could happen to her. No, never!

'I despise you!' The words rang out and she didn't care who overheard them. 'Love you, Sheik Khasim? I should hope I have too much pride and taste to love a man like you!'

'An Arab?' The words came soft and purring from his lips.

'Yes,' she said it defiantly. 'You're as barbaric as the desert you live in—all your education and your command of languages doesn't make you civilised!'

'Exactly so, Diane.'

She caught her breath as his meaning sank deep into her sensibilities like a barb. She looked around wildly, but all she saw were his people and the taut black tents of the *douar*, and beyond them the limitless miles of desert, shimmering a hot gold under the burning orb of the sun. She was trapped like a moth in amber, and the Sheik watched lazily as she backed away from him until, with a gasp, she found herself against the royal-blue walls of his tent.

He smiled as he approached her, but not in the way he had smiled at the Beni-Haran woman. He reached out and his arm hooked itself about her waist and as if she weighed no more than the Beni-Haran child he lifted her and carried her inside the tent, held her a moment and then dropped her to the big floor cushions.

'This is the way it must be—*Kismet*,' he said.

'*Le droit du Seigneur!*' she flung back at him, crouched upon the cushions beneath the arrogant spread of his legs in the leather boots, deep in the nap of the carpet.

'*D'accord, bint*. The right of the master to do exactly what he pleases with the woman in his power. It's as well that you know what to expect!'

'How could I look at you, *mon Arabe*, and not know?' Diane braved his look, but inwardly she was quaking from a mixture of fears. A woman had little defence against most men and this one was formidable in his lean strength of body, in his hatred of the Ronays, made so manifest by the cicatrice that carved its way into his face.

He was the Caid ... the Seigneur, and he could do as he pleased with her. If she screamed for help, those who heard her cries would ignore them. If she pleaded for his mercy, he would enjoy making a beggar of her. If she wept he would say that passion was meant to be watered by a woman's tears.

An Arab, it was said, could carve a quotation on every stone in the desert, and when Diane looked at Khasim ben Haran she saw that unrelenting hatred had slashed deep as the sabre into his flesh.

'Attend to your face with some grease,' he said curtly, 'otherwise you will resemble a half-skinned peach. Then rest upon the couch and read a book if you wish—I have right now more important matters than a woman to attend to.'

He swung upon his heel and upon leaving the tent released the flap so Diane was shut inside its shadowy coolness. As he left he was whistling a section of music, softly, melodiously and perfectly in tune. *Che mi frena in tal momento.* What restrains me in such a moment?

With a helpless little cry Diane covered her face with her hands and sank down among the cushions. She tried to stop thinking about him, but his invasion of her mind was almost total. There seemed not a single escape route for her to follow that would bring relief from images of him; the deep menacing tones of his voice had lodged in her very eardrums.

'Brute ... devil!' In her despair she pummelled a cushion with her fist and wished it were his cruel, scarred face. 'I hate you ... hate you ... hate you!'

But did a mocking voice whisper that hate was sometimes only a kiss away from love?

As the whisper slid through her mind Diane had an image of herself arched over a brown strong arm, her struggling limbs subdued and her lips forced to yield to kisses she could only imagine as pitiless. Kisses and— and other intimacies she didn't dare to think about!

She had to get hold of a horse as soon as possible ... *Dieu*, what a headstrong idiot she had been to ride alone in the desert, yet how could she have dreamed that fate meant her to meet Khasim ben Haran ... she hadn't known that such a man existed!

No man had ever got close enough to kiss her, but here in this tent she was surrounded by the masculine belongings of a man. She breathed the lingering smoke of the Sheik's tobacco, the tang of his horses and his leather accoutrements. She had brushed her hair with his hairbrush, and had slept in his bed!

It was all strangely dreamlike, and yet on the edge of nightmare. Outside the sun was beating down on the black tents, into which most of the occupants had withdrawn while the afternoon heat was so overpowering. She had lain on those sands and felt the sun branding her, and the next time she faced the desert she must ensure that she had water, a robe to cover her head, and a swift horse. Given those and a dash of luck she might get safely back to Brittany.

Perhaps from that safe distance it might be interesting to remember the Arab with the scarred cheek, but just now he was too disturbing to think about.

Just now the desert seemed to her less merciless than the Sheik of the Beni-Haran.

CHAPTER FOUR

DIANE stirred awake and knew at once that it was the aroma of mint tea which had awoken her. She blinked until her eyes cleared and expected to see Achmed with the tea tray, but when she glanced upwards she was startled to find herself looking at an unveiled Arabian girl.

The girl leaned downwards and intently studied Diane; she was almost barbaric in her beauty, her arching dark brows meeting like scimitars above eyes of a deep glistening brown. Dark plaits were looped beneath the snood that she wore and tiny ringlets of hair were curled beside her high cheekbones; her nose was thin and shapely, her lips red and full. Against the velvet of her amber dress there hung a necklace of gold beads and a small golden crescent; her eyelids were dusted with kohl and there was henna on her tapering hands. Diane couldn't help noticing the deep lustre which the kohl gave to the girl's eyes, adding to her seductive quality.

Suddenly she smiled, but not in a friendly way. 'So you are the *roumia* my lord keeps in his tent.' The language was French but the accent was huskily Arabian. 'I believed I would find a beauty so raving that it would account for his unaccustomed interest in one of your milk-skinned race. But you aren't beautiful at all! You have hair like a boy and the skin is peeling from your nose and forehead.'

The girl stood back from the divan and placing her hands on rounded hips she stood and laughed mockingly at Diane. Her teeth were perfect, shining white against the deep honey of her skin. Diane couldn't help staring; she had heard that some Arabian girls when young were incredibly lovely, and this one lived up to the description. It struck Diane as absurd that anyone so lovely should feel jealous of another woman.

She sat up, smoothing a hand over her ruffled hair and very aware that she looked awkward and untidy after falling asleep on the divan. The pot of mint tea stood on the divan table, along with cups and a plate of small cakes studded with sultanas.

'The tea is for me?' Diane felt strangely nervous of the girl.

'Achmed brought in the tray—I am not a servant.'

'Of course not.' Diane leaned forward to use the sugar tongs. 'Will you join me in a cup of tea?'

'My lord Khasim asked for tea to be brought to his tent; it isn't for a woman to proceed until he appears.'

'The tea could be cold by then.' Diane lifted the pot and filled her own cup with the aromatic brew. 'You might as well join me, you know. The Sheik Khasim doesn't expect me to behave like an Arabian woman, waiting patiently until he deigns to appear.'

'I will wait because I am Arabian.' The girl sank down gracefully on one of the big floor cushions, the slim chains on her ankles making a musical sound as she crossed her legs and sat odalisque-style. She had, Diane thought, the sinuous grace of a dancer, and her display of jealousy combined with her deference towards the Sheik indicated that she was someone who entertained him . . . in more ways than one, Diane decided cynically.

Diane sipped her tea and rather liked its fragrance; in any case she was thirsty, being unaccustomed as yet to the dry air of the desert.

'At least have a cake,' she said to the girl, hoping to distract her from staring so curiously at every atom of her person, from her hair down to her bare feet. She couldn't seem to keep the low-backed Eastern slippers on her feet, which looked very white in contrast to the other girl's honey-hued skin.

'It is impolite for a woman to taste the food before a man does.' The girl's French was singsong and attractively husky to the ear, and as she spoke she held her hands together at the fingertips. She had, Diane thought, the manners and appearance of a girl who had been especially taught to please a man; there was something about her of a doll rather than a spontaneous human being. Incredibly lovely and yet at the same time as unnerving as a puppet that walked and talked ... at the behest of someone who controlled her actions.

Diane poured herself some more tea and began to wish that the Sheik would arrive. Instinctively she knew that like a *geisha* this girl's only function was to be slavishly attentive to a man. His every wish was her command, and now she found in that man's tent a strange female who threatened her status as the Sheik's plaything.

The brown eyes probed as if seeking the source of Diane's attraction. 'Is it the colour of your skin which he likes?' she demanded suddenly. 'Yasmina told me that your skin under your chemise is like goat's milk.'

'I don't believe Yasmina said anything about goats.' Diane had to smile. 'She seems a kind person.'

'What use is kindness?' The sensuous red lips twisted scornfully. 'She will be married to some ordinary man and will be nothing more than the keeper of his house.'

'Perhaps Yasmina prefers that to the dubious honour of being a rich man's *kadine*. Surely a *kadine* lasts only as long as she is found distracting, afterwards she is either neglected or passed on to some other man who prefers the passing fancy to an established woman in his life?'

The lustrous brown eyes grew hard in the barbaric prettiness of the girl's face. 'A *kadine* can establish herself with the highest in the land if she has the looks and the ability to be always pleasing, and knows how to outwit her rivals.'

The words hung in the air between the two girls, one as fair-skinned as the other was dark; one as eager to escape the Sheik's arms as the other was eager to remain in them.

Diane could feel her heart beating so fast it made her feel breathless and a little faint. She reached for a cake and ate it, building up the strength she mustn't lose ... not now!

'What is your name?' she asked quietly.

'I am called Hiriz—it means to charm.' The girl swept her eyes over Diane. 'I cannot see how you could charm my lord. He has no time for *boys*.'

'I'm utterly sure of that,' Diane dryly agreed. She studied Hiriz and knew, excitedly, that she had found someone in the *douar* who would be only too pleased to help her get away from it. Unlike Yasmina this girl was far from timid and under the sway of a brother ... she was under the sway of a passion which had nothing to do with family or tribal loyalty.

Diane leaned forward, holding the girl's gaze with her own. She didn't forget what the Sheik had said about her eyes ... that to his superstitious people blue eyes belonged to a witch who could cast spells. 'Hiriz, I want to get away from the Sheik Khasim—will you help me? Will you get me a horse and one or two other things that I need in order to make my escape from the *douar*? With me gone from the Sheik's tent, you will be his sole in-

terest again, won't you? You know I'm a rival while I
remain here.'

Hiriz gazed at Diane as if mesmerised, then she took a
swift look at the tent opening, which remained firmly in
place. 'You truly wish to leave the *douar*?' There was a
note of incredulity in her voice, though she spoke in low-
tones. 'You have no desire to be with my lord Khasim?'

Diane shook her head firmly. 'I want to go home to
my family—surely it will be to your advantage, Hiriz, to
help me.'

'It will not be to my advantage if the Sheik Khasim
should find out that I have helped you flee from him.'
The girl stroked a thoughtful finger along her slanting
eyebrows, the bangles sliding along her arm, the perfume
on her skin drifting to Diane, a mixture of roses and
musk. 'He can show great anger and I am but a woman—
he might break my neck in his strong hands, and I ask
myself if you are worth such a risk.'

'If I stay here,' Diane said deliberately, 'he'll forget you
while he amuses himself with me. If you love him, Hiriz,
how will you be able to stand it, knowing that someone
else is in his arms, receiving his kisses and his caresses?'

Hiriz caught her breath sharply, her eyes sliding from
Diane's lips down her body to her slim ankles, one of
them still bandaged.

'You might not think me attractive,' Diane went on,
'but your Sheik wouldn't keep me in his tent, would he, if
he found me unappealing? It probably is my skin and
hair that attracts him. Perhaps he feels the need for a
change and has grown bored with dark hair and honey
skin, not to mention the docility of women who always
surrender to him because he's the powerful Caid of the
Beni-Haran. In me, Hiriz, he doesn't find this docility—
he has to subdue me and he enjoys it.'

'Don't you enjoy being subdued by him?' Hiriz wanted to know, her hennaed fingers locked together in a kind of torment.

'Of course I don't,' Diane said spiritedly. 'I'm not that kind of woman, to be forced into bowing and scraping to a man. It means nothing to me that he's the lord of this part of the desert.'

'But he's a man in every way—he's tall and strong, he can ride like the wind, throw a lance so it sings through the air, wrestle with any one of his soldiers and pin them down in the sands. He can hunt and hawk, and he became chief of the Beni-Haran when he was only twenty, when his father died from typhus. Older men wanted the leadership but my lord Khasim took and held it. He has wisdom and force of character, and a woman is honoured when he desires to find his ease with her.'

'In my country,' Diane explained, 'a man doesn't pick and choose women for his pleasure as if they're so many peaches on a tree. I know it's the custom with your people, but mine have a different arrangement. The women are more independent and it isn't permitted for a man to carry off a woman for his—enjoyment. It's against the law!'

'Even so,' a smile curved on the girl's lush mouth, 'it is more exciting when men are lawless towards women. It is forbidden for an Arab to look with passion upon the wife, sister or daughter of another man, but it happens and clandestine meetings take place. Passion in the desert is strong, fierce, but it is known by the Beni-Haran that my lord Khasim does not punish lovers as severely as others do. The use of the whip is forbidden except in the case of child molesters and those who mistreat their animals. The man who makes love to another man's woman is fined a sheep or a goat and sometimes a horse, which is handed over to the husband or father of the woman involved.'

'And what punishment is meted out to the erring wife?' Diane asked curiously.

'She is warned by the Sheik Khasim that if she goes astray again she will be cast out from the tribe. This is the worst that could happen to any one of us. To be of the Beni-Haran is to be part of one of the oldest and most princely tribes of Arabia. We were established in the desert when the three wise men followed the star to Bethlehem. We have fought many enemies, and in one of the wars we were part of the army which was led by Lurens of Arabia.'

'Lawrence,' Diane murmured to herself, a British soldier and a great hero who had died tragically in England.

Suddenly Hiriz leaned confidentially close to Diane. 'There is some mystery connected to my lord Khasim's mother. It is said that she came from a faraway country called Russia. His father came upon her in the desert of Dimashk where it is said she was being sold as a slave. His father always called her Barishnaya—at the *kasbah* there is a painting of her, and my lady Morgana, who is sister to the Sheik, is the image of her, with eyes more slanting dark than mine.'

Diane was intrigued, but she didn't intend to lose sight of her main objective, which was to enlist this girl's aid in getting away from the Beni-Haran. Had she been merely a guest here, then she could have found much to interest her in these attractive people who lived much as they had done in Biblical times.

'Hiriz, all you need do is get me a horse, a bottle of water, and some kind of robe. I'm sure you don't wish to share the Sheik with me, but that will happen unless I manage to get away within the next twenty-four hours—all that is holding his hand right now is the fact that I'm still suffering some of the effects of sunburn. I have to leave before he——' Diane broke off, biting her lip. 'I'm not like you, Hiriz. I'm not in love with him.'

'You have a man in your own country?' This, for Hiriz, seemed the only explanation. She seemed unable to comprehend that any woman could shrink from the arms of the Sheik.

'Yes, my grandfather,' Diane said simply. 'I'm all he has left—he'll be terribly lonely without me.'

'I—I don't know if I dare assist you.' Hiriz wrung her hennaed hands together as she knelt there on the floor cushion, the lamplight blending with the amber of her dress and the honey of her skin. She was pretty, indulged, and afraid of punishment. With her head bent she looked almost childlike, but Diane sensed that she was well versed in the art of pleasing a man. She had probably been trained by the harem mistress at the *kasbah*; the Sheik wouldn't reside in the desert without the pleasant distractions of a *kadine*.

'Help me,' Diane pleaded. 'The Sheik won't punish you—you're far too pretty and he obviously likes women.' Diane recalled the charm of his smile when he had saved the little Arab boy from choking. 'You're special to him, aren't you, Hiriz? What we call in my country his sweetheart.'

'I play the zither for him, and I dance—yes, I love him,' Hiriz said fiercely. 'I sit at his knee and watch his face as he talks—he must soon take a wife, and I would die to be his wife!'

'That would defeat your purpose——' Diane broke off, remembering that the Sheik had said the same to her. 'Don't let me stand in your way—I might, you know.'

'You?' Hiriz raised jealous eyes to Diane. 'My lord Khasim wouldn't marry a foreign woman—a *roumia*!'

'His father did,' Diane carefully fed the flames of the girl's jealousy, 'if the story about his mother is true.'

'His mother was beautiful.' Hiriz leapt to her feet with the agility of a young cat, her chains and bangles making a barbaric jangle. 'She had dark waving hair like his sister, slanting eyes with long black lashes—you aren't beautiful in the way our men like!' Hiriz tensed her hands and menaced Diane with long fingers dyed to the knuckle in henna. 'You are witch-eyed, your skin peels in the sun and you have the shape of a boy—a goat herder!'

'Nonetheless, I'm here in the tent of your Sheik,' Diane said pointedly. 'He gave me his bed to sleep in and he has said I'm to be taken to the court of the seven fountains.'

'To sweep the yard?' Hiriz laughed, but her eyes were uncertain as she cast a glance at the scarlet hanging which separated the lounging area of the Sheik's tent from the more intimate area where he slept. 'I suppose I could fetch you a horse, *roumia*, and water for your journey. You have cast a spell over my lord Khasim with your witch-eyes, that can be the only reason why he keeps you here.'

'Of course it is.' Diane could feel herself relaxing at last. 'I need a good swift horse, Hiriz, and he must be saddled so I can ride off without hindrance.'

'Will you know in which direction to ride?' Hiriz asked. 'The desert is a place of great distances and already you have been lost in it, and would have died there had my lord Khasim not found you.'

'I know.' Diane brooded a moment on the problem that faced her in the desert; she could but hope that she would find her way to Dar-Arisi, or meet up with friendly nomads who would show her the way. At least she would not be facing the kind of danger Khasim ben Haran represented, and that was all that mattered to her right now. She wouldn't be used by him to satisfy a cruel need to be revenged ... she wouldn't be forced to give herself to him, to be degraded and left without pride in herself. It wasn't because he was an Arab that she shrank from him ... it was because he was driven by hatred for the grandfather she loved. She couldn't endure the thought of being in his arms and feeling cruelty on the lips that kissed her into submission to him.

'You have nerve, *roumia*.' Hiriz spoke with grudging respect. 'I would sooner give myself to a man than face the dangers of the desert. Perhaps you are afraid of men, eh?'

'I—I never had cause to be afraid until I met your Sheik——' Diane broke off, steeling her nerves as the tent flap was swept aside, giving entrance to the tall cloaked figure of the Sheik. His eyes flashed from one girl to the other as he unbuckled his great cloak and flung it off. Sand grains fell from its folds and there was a layer of dust on his high boots.

'My lord has had a hard ride?' Hiriz touched the sleeve of his tunic and gazed up at him with such candid admiration that Diane could understand his lordly assumption that all women were ready to fall at his feet.

'We have been to examine one of the wells,' he explained, and his brows were drawn into a black line above his eyes. 'Someone has spoiled the water by tipping salt into the well and I have a strong suspicion who the culprits might be. The Ab-Asha tribe have claimed that well as theirs for a long time, but I happen to know for certain that the Beni-Haran have territorial rights to it.

It's a nasty little game to play and I have left men to stand guard over the well. No one must drink from it until it has been pumped out and purified. Salt! Of all things for someone to drink salted water in the desert! The Ab-Asha will be made to pay!'

His gaze settled on the tea-tray. 'Is that pot of tea still hot?' he demanded of Diane.

She touched it and found that the tea had grown lukewarm. She shook her head in answer to him, her eyes upon his angry face, the scar cruelly outlined against the sun-bronzed skin.

'It will suffice,' he said. 'Please to pour me a cup.'

'May I help my lord remove his boots?' Hiriz said seductively.

He shrugged and sprawled on the divan while the girl knelt at his feet and tugged off his boots. 'Be careful of my spurs,' he said to her. 'I don't want you to cut yourself.'

'My lord is always thoughtful of Hiriz.' She smiled at him seductively and when the boots were removed she fitted low-backed slippers to his feet. Diane watched the performance and didn't know whether to be amused or scornful of the way he accepted the attention like some Oriental pasha. She supposed he was used to it, a man with a harem at his beck and call.

She handed him a cup of tea which he drank almost in a gulp. 'I was obliged to taste that salted water,' he grimaced. 'Another cup of tea would be most welcome, Diane.'

Hiriz glanced jealously at Diane when he used her name, and she sidled closer to him and one of her slim hands touched his knee possessively. He glanced down at her indulgently ... an adoring toy for his amusement, the kind of creature he meant to make of *her*, Diane thought resentfully. Still only half-confident that Hiriz would keep her promise and provide her with a horse, she decided to annoy the girl by stealing some of the Sheik's attention.

'What will you do with the man who salted the well, Sheik Khasim?' She held his gaze with her blue eyes as she handed him a second cup of tea. 'I expect the punishment will fit the crime?'

'*D'accord.*' He tossed the mint tea down his throat. 'A few sips of that stuff has parched my throat, so he'll be made to drink a little more of it and then he will be sent back to the Ab-Asha without a water-bottle. That will teach him not to play tricks with the most precious commodity in the desert.'

Diane held out the plate of sultana cakes so the Sheik could take one, and she couldn't help but agree that water was precious in the desert when she remembered her own parched agony and how delicious the lemonade had tasted when he had knelt beside her on the sands, kind to her in his autocratic way until he discovered that her name was Ronay.

As he bit into a cake his eyes played their dark lights over Diane's hair, travelling down to where her dress opened at the neck to reveal the soft skin which the sun of his desert had scorched. She tried to control the upsurge of a blush, but it swept over her as relentlessly as his eyes, making her not only aware of her own body but of the lithe maleness of the Sheik's lounging figure on the divan, the Arabian girl clinging to him as if she loved every aspect of his ownership of her.

Hiriz flung a look at Diane. 'Will my lord wish *her* to dance for him in future?' she demanded.

He laughed softly and took another cake, biting it in half with his firm white teeth. 'The British *bint* doesn't number among her skills the ones that belong to Hiriz,' he replied. 'I very much doubt if she could hold a ruby in her navel, *berida*, or move her hips to the beat of the desert drums. On the other hand I believe she knows which end of a gun to fire, and she may have a good riding seat.'

'The skills of a boy!' Hiriz tossed her head scornfully. 'My lord surprises me that he admires these things in a woman—if she is one!'

His amused eyes held Diane's even as his fingers lightly fondled the shoulder of Hiriz. 'What have you to say to that?' he asked her. 'Are you a woman—in the true sense of the word, I mean, not merely that you possess the body of one, slender but discernible as female?'

Diane bit her lip in an effort to hold back her temper. She didn't wish to lose it in front of Hiriz; she wanted the other girl's jealousy to be fuelled to burning point.

'I'm sure, Sheik Khasim, that with your knowledge of women you must be aware of whether or not I appeal to your masculine feelings. Nature has so arranged it, or so I'm told.'

His eyes narrowed but his lip twitched as if he suppressed the urge to smile. 'So you have a sense of humour, *bint*?'

'It's making a recovery,' she rejoined.

'I'm gratified to hear it. Spirit and humour become a woman as much as pearls around her neck.'

'Pearls?' Hiriz scanned the Sheik's face. 'They are for a bride!'

'Are they, my bit of sugar?' He lounged back against a silk-striped cushion and his fingers slid away from the girl's shoulder. His eyes were intent upon Diane, as if he were wondering why all at once she took this almost

flirtatious line with him. Her heart raced; he was shrewd
and alert, and she prayed that he wouldn't guess that she
was deliberately egging Hiriz on to help her get away
from him.

'In my country pearls are for tears,' Diane explained.
'Many brides avoid wearing them for that reason.'

Hiriz gave her a smouldering look, which Diane returned with a cool smile.

'I hope to see you dance, Hiriz. Do you really hold a
ruby in your navel? How do you manage it, with
muscle control?'

'Hiriz has danced from a small child.' There was a note
of amusement in the Sheik's voice, and his mention of
her name drew the girl's eyes to his face, lustrous with
kohl and a look of longing he seemed, to Diane, to take
rather for granted. 'Tonight, little one, you will dance
for the *lalla* and myself. I feel the need for some enter-
tainment after that annoying business of the well. Graceful as a young gazelle, aren't you?'

'Does my lord truly think so?' The girl pressed to him
and raised a hand as if to stroke his face. He caught her
wrist in his fingers and studied the henna that stained
her skin.

'Why do you use this stuff, Hiriz? Your hands look as
if they have been dipped in a chicken.'

'It is to make them pretty——'

'You aren't an Ouled-Nail,' he said crisply. 'You are
pretty enough without staining yourself with kohl and
henna. Make less use of them in future.'

Hiriz pouted her red lips at him. 'I do it to please my
lord. I live for you and will do anything to give you joy.'
The girl lowered her forehead to the back of his hand,
and he gave her an absent kind of caress, as if she were a
kitten snuggling close for his attention. At the same time

he glanced at Diane, who sat quietly watching the scene. She was so absorbed that she couldn't look away when he caught her gaze, she could only think to herself that they looked like one of the illustrated woodcuts in her grandfather's beautifully bound copy of the *Arabian Nights Treasury*. The two profiles were cut with precision, their skin tones were those of the desert sands, and the girl's curvaceous arms seemed as if made to entwine about the Sheik's firm brown neck.

'What thoughts are in hiding in those blue eyes?' he asked. 'Their mystery intrigues me and makes me wonder what I would see if I could penetrate them.'

'Blue eyes aren't mysterious; it's dark ones that hold secrets.'

'Day and night,' he mused. 'All the same, when one looks up at the sky it's impossible to see beyond that blueness; when a man dives into the sea it is only possible for him to go so deep without risking his life. A flame, a diamond, and lightning hold elements of blue, and each has an elusive quality—and a certain danger.'

'I had heard,' she said, 'that Arabs could carve a profound statement on every stone in the desert, and that you can read riddles in the sand.'

'To a certain extent it's true, Diane. Would you like me to send for the *sorcier* so he might read the riddle of your destiny in the sand?'

'I thought you were the master of my destiny,' she rejoined.

'*Touché.*' He inclined his head and there was dark and fascinating brilliance to his eyes that Diane couldn't evade; she somehow had the feeling that he was enjoying himself. 'I have aroused your feminine curiosity, have I not? You wish to find out if the sand diviner can tell you what lies in store for you.'

'I'd be a fool, Sheik Khasim, if I didn't know that. Haven't you spelled it out for me without the aid of a bag of sand?'

'All the same——' He suddenly arose from the divan, spilling Hiriz to the floor cushions, and strode to the tent flaps. He flicked them aside and called Achmed's name and when his manservant quickly appeared the Sheik gave him some instructions in the deep-throated Arabic, not a graceful language but commanding and fierce. When the flap dropped into place the tall figure of the Sheik swung round and stood there against the deep blue, powerful and sure of himself, and in the mood to be amused by the two girls who in every possible way contrasted with each other.

He swept his gaze from one to the other and his smile, made slightly menacing by his scar, changed to a lazy laugh. He came to the divan table and leaned down to take a *cigarro* from the carved box. It jutted darkly from his lips as he lit it, and he stood braced on long hard legs in the Arab trousers that were tight at the calf, the figure of Hiriz still on the floor, reclining there, sulky-mouthed as she gazed up at him.

'I should like my fortune read,' she said.

'Your fortune is in your face, my bit of sugar.'

'My face is pleasing to my lord?' She knelt and wrapped an arm about his left leg, resting her cheek against the hard thrust of his calf muscles. He permitted the embrace, the smoke of his *cigarro* slipping lazily from his lips. Diane regarded Hiriz with a look of disdain; how could she make it so slavishly obvious that she adored every living inch of him? Diane couldn't imagine what it felt like to be so sensuously hungry for a man that nothing mattered except to be part of him. To Diane it looked like a form of abasement and she scorned it ... the day or night would never come when she would grovel at a man's feet. She'd have to be whipped into such a submission!

Her eyes blazed proudly as she allowed them to run all the way up the Sheik's hard frame to his face ... the moment she met his eyes she knew that he had divined what she was thinking.

'The desert may in time, *bint*, make you less inhibited,' he drawled. 'It has an insidious effect upon the coolest temperament; ice cannot help but melt when subjected to our sort of climate, and you may find yourself melting even as you try to resist the forces of nature.'

'Is that where you like women, in a resistless heap at your feet?' Diane flung out a scornful hand towards Hiriz. 'Doesn't it get boring for you, having a menagerie of women who collapse into submission the moment you look at them?'

His eyes, clouded about by *cigarro* smoke, brooded upon Diane's face. His gaze moved to the wings of fair hair that revealed her ears and travelled along the pale parting at the centre of her hair. A page-boy style that somehow intensified the wide shape of her eyes and the density of their blueness, set off by clustering lashes darker toned than the rest of her colouring.

His gaze dropped to her lips and dwelt there so intently that all at once Diane was divining the trend of his thoughts. Her right hand pressed nervously against her body ... she hadn't yet put miles of desert sand between herself and this man, she was still captive in his tent and while she remained so was still at the mercy of his inclinations. No matter how she fought and clawed, matched against his vigour she would stand no chance at all. The taunting knowledge of it was there in his eyes for her to see and she had to fight a frightened urge to cower away from him. She hated him for his physical effect upon her, and despised herself for the fears that seemed to go shooting through her very bones when she looked at him and saw the virile power in his body.

He was out to make a craven of her, Diane Ronay, and she drew on every ounce of her courage in order to look squarely at him without displaying her inward turmoil.

'One thing is certain, *bint*,' he spoke in a deliberate tone of voice, 'I don't expect to be bored by you.'

'Am I supposed to take that as a compliment or a warning?' She flung up her chin defiantly, yet was aware with every cringing nerve of the firmness of his tawny skin over the muscles of his arms and chest. He was like a tiger, alert and alive to the very depth of his agile body ... alarming even at a distance.

'You're intelligent enough to take it as both,' he said. 'That grandfather of yours has treated you like a boy, but I shan't. He has taught you to be fearless even when you are quaking at the knees; it must have been something of a disappointment for him that you were not born a boy.'

'I wish I had been!' At this moment Diane wished it with a fervency she couldn't hide. 'I wouldn't be here with you, would I?'

'Not in your present capacity,' he laughed softly. There was a movement at the flap of the tent and he turned to give entrance to a gnarled figure in a green turban and a kaftan who carried in one hand a stick shaped like a serpent. He bowed to the Sheik, who inclined his head in return and at the same time took hold of Hiriz and drew her to her feet. He said something to her in Arabic and she scowled and shot a look of animosity at Diane.

'Go, child,' the Sheik urged her out of the tent. 'Take a rest so you will dance your best later this evening.'

'I want to stay and hear what the diviner reads in the sand for the *roumia*.' Hiriz hung back and fixed pleading eyes on his face. 'I won't be treated like a child——'

'What else are you?' he teased, pushing her outside the tent. 'Begone, and wash some of the paint off your face and hands.'

He drew the tent flap firmly in place and turned to face the sand diviner. 'For the sake of amusement, Batouch, I wish you to read the sand grains for the *lalla*. She is interested in finding out what experiences await her in the desert.'

Diane shot him a burning look as she caught the note of irony in his voice. She wanted to contradict his statement that she was interested in such nonsense as sand divining, but already the old man had taken a skin bag from an inner pocket of his kaftan. He indicated the divan table and when the Sheik inclined his head the diviner pulled loose the drawstring of the bag and emptied its contents upon the surface of the table. The Sheik removed the tea tray in order to provide more space, and then he watched the proceedings, a booted leg at rest upon the edge of the divan, a lean brown hand relaxed upon his knee.

With the serpent shaped stick Batouch moved the sand around on the table top, then suddenly he looked at Diane and asked her in guttural French to re-shape the sand with her hands. She hesitated, but his gaze was insistent and, with a slight shrug, she leaned forward and did as he requested. The sand, she noticed, was in several different shades as if it came from different parts of the desert. Some of it was almost black, some of it pink and orange contrasting with the tawny shades. It felt velvety to the touch and she had the oddest sensation in her fingers, as if she were forming it into patterns not of her own volition. All the time the old man in the Meccan green turban watched her, as did the Sheik, his lean face curiously intent.

It was a lot of nonsense, she told herself, yet all the same she could feel her heart beating excitedly and there was undoubtedly a tingling sensation in the tips of her fingers. Suddenly the sand felt as if it were burning her, as it had in the desert yesterday; growing hot beneath the merciless rays of the sun. But here they were inside the blue tent and the sun outside had softened as dusk slowly drew its veils over the desert. She drew back from the table and stemmed an absurd impulse to dip her tingling fingers in the little bowl of water which had been provided with the cakes; a custom, she had noticed, among the Arabs.

Batouch nodded as if he knew that the sand had imparted this peculiar sensation to her fingers, then he leaned over the table and stared intently at the patterns she had made. He began to mutter to himself, but in Arabic so Diane was at a loss to understand him. She glanced at the Sheik, whose brows were drawn together as he listened to the diviner muttering to himself. Suddenly the old man pointed at Diane, making her start back nervously. He spoke to her in Arabic and she glanced at the Sheik so he could translate the words for her. But he was frowning and staring at the old man and abruptly he asked him a question. The diviner then pointed at the sand where it was darkly patched and formed into a mound, and the Sheik shook his head and seemed to deny the diviner's assertion.

'What does he say?' Diane felt a strange sense of foreboding. 'Even if it's nonsense I'd like to know——'

The Sheik looked at her and an instant before he shrugged his shoulders she saw a look of uncertainty in his eyes. 'As you say, a lot of amusing nonsense and nothing more. He says a dark stranger has crossed your path, but we both know that already, don't we?'

'Is that all he meant?' Diane dragged her gaze from the Sheik and looked at the sand diviner. Abruptly it occurred to her that he had earlier spoken some French and at once she asked him in the Gallic tongue what he had seen in the sand that seemed to trouble him. He stared at her and she saw from his eyes that he understood her words ... he was about to answer her question when the Sheik uttered a single commanding word. Diane knew instantly that the old man had been ordered to remain silent.

'How dare you?' Her eyes blazed at the Sheik. 'Allow him to answer me or I shall think you have something to hide. What the devil is all the mystery?'

She hadn't wanted to believe in any of this, but Grandpère had once told her that some of the elderly Arabs who travelled the roads to Mecca and Samarkand were mystics who could perform strange tricks and had the gift of clairvoyancy. Things that occurred in the desert weren't to be lightly dismissed; he had himself witnessed a mirage and seen as if in a great pool a distant town reflected upside down: he and his men hadn't reached that town until nightfall, but several of them had witnessed that inverted reflection.

'You were the one who wanted the diviner to read the sand grains for me,' Diane flung at the Sheik. 'I have a right to know what he has seen.'

'Then know it!' The Sheik compressed his nostrils. 'He has seen a grave!'

Diane made a convulsive little noise in her throat. 'Whose?' she managed to ask.

'Whose do you think?' He stared a long hard moment

into her frightened eyes and then gave a cynical smile, a twist of the lips that didn't reach his eyes. 'Mine, of course.'

'Yours?' Diane had reached for her hammering throat and could feel the pulse beating against her fingers. 'I—I don't believe you—how could it be when Batouch was reading the sands for me?'

'You are here with me, are you not? Here in my camp, my tent. The strands of our fates have interwoven and Batouch has glimpsed part of the pattern. It is surely simple enough to understand?'

'I—I wish to ask Batouch.' She turned to the diviner and spoke to him again in French, and yet again the Sheik ordered him not to answer her.

'It's enough that I tell you,' he said arrogantly, and bending forward he swept the sand grains together in a heap, the shadings mingling and no longer forming a discernible shape. He spoke in gentler tones to the old man, who inclined his head and carefully replaced the grains in his drawstring bag. Before he left the tent the Sheik gave him several coins, which he tucked away with a salaam, his deepset eyes flicking across Diane's face as he bowed himself out of the tent, the flap falling slowly in place behind his green-turbaned figure.

Diane swept her eyes up and down the tall figure of the Sheik. It seemed impossible to imagine someone so vital and alive struck into the stillness of death ... it was something she ought to wish for, and yet to contemplate an end to all that power and authority seemed to send a chill through her body, right down to the bottom of her spine until she shivered.

'Don't do that.' He suddenly leaned down and closed warm hands upon her shoulders. 'I meant the divining to be taken as a game——'

'I'm glad you found it amusing.' She tried to shake free
of his touch, but instantly his hands tightened and with
barely any effort he brought her to her feet so she was
close to him. He locked his left arm about her waist and
tilted back her head with his other hand, forcing her to
look upwards into his eyes. Dark, brilliant, with a sensuous slant to them, the lashes clustering along the lids. He
held her and watched her while her heart pounded and
then she felt his hands slip down her arms to her wrists
and grip them. Instantly she wanted to escape and reacted
by trying to pull herself away from him. Her alarm
agitated the devil in his eyes, and he murmured :

'I believe our *tournament d'amour* begins, *chérie*,' and
again with ease he lifted and flung her to the divan so her
limbs sprawled like those of a doll. He laughed softly
and his lean menacing face was right above her. 'You see
how easy it is, little one? What is a woman when she
comes up against a man?'

'A man?' Diane's lips were shaking, but she made a
proud effort not to show how helpless he made her feel
as he watched narrowly the expression on her face. She
glared back at him, a cat in a trap who would claw him
if only her hands were free to do so, but he had hold of
them in one large strong hand and with the other he
stroked the hair from her brow and trailed his fingers
down her cheek to the edge of her mouth.

'All right,' she hissed, 'if you're going to rape me, then
do it and be done!'

'Are you that eager?' he drawled, and he played over
her a look which seemed to remove the clothes from her
body.

'You know very well what I am,' she choked. 'I hate
the very touch of you—you barbarian!'

'Then let me touch you some more,' he mocked, and

his hand slid down and fondled her shoulder, slid lower until it hovered near her agitated breast. 'The prudery of the virgin is always exciting——'

'Have you ravished many of them?' she panted, straining to keep her body out of reach of his lean dark fingers, on fire with a fury and a fear she felt to the far reaches of her body. All the rest of the world seemed to have receded and all there was for Diane was a blue tent and the savage gold of an Arab's skin, giving off a warmth that touched her own.

'You have a reckless tongue, Diane, and I shall leash it for you if you aren't careful.' He leaned closer and his touch was teasing, featherlight on her body. His pupils had dilated and there was a flare to his nostrils—the rather uneven way he breathed made Diane catch her own breath. She wasn't so innocent that she didn't know what was happening to him ... he was getting out of control and she felt as if his eyes were consuming her, a prelude to being engulfed like ... like a moth in a flame.

'Y-you wouldn't behave like this with an Arabian girl,' she protested.

'Of course not.' He gave a laugh that sounded as cruel as it was mocking. 'With you and me, chérie, it's an eye for an eye, a woman for a woman. As I've already intimated, when I want something I don't allow petty scruples to stand in my way.'

'Petty?' she breathed. 'You want to ruin my life and you call it that? You haven't an ounce of mercy in you ... you're every inch the sort who expects a woman to kiss the hand you strike her with.'

'I don't feel like striking you, little one.' His fingers teased the soft skin of her neck. 'My inclination right now is to stroke you—your skin, you know, is ravissante. I had all but forgotten what it felt like to hold in my arms a girl of profound modesty—pure as the driven snow. Struggle, my *bint*, it makes a pleasing change from obedient servility.'

'You brute devil,' she gasped. 'Lecher—kidnapper— damned Arab!'

'Go on,' he taunted, 'let it out of your system. When the blood is hot the pain is less.'

'Pain?' Her eyes flared wide with shocked recognition of what he meant.

'All our pleasures have to be paid for, one way or another,' he taunted.

'Y-you think I could find *that*, with you?' She was breathing quickly through her mouth, feeling even as she fought him the tightening pressure of his hard warm arms around her, forcing her into a slim taut arch that wouldn't yield to him.

'What does it matter,' his lips hovered above hers, 'so long as I get what I want?'

She fought crazedly with him but found his lean body alive with a strength that made her struggles a breathless futility. Snarling something in Arabic, he tipped her helplessly across his arm and the heat of his lips burned upon hers, a searing flame that swept her skin from throat to toe. For an eternity of unimaginable moments Diane was lost in the deep fires of his kiss ... blistering her emotions as the sun had blistered her skin in the relentless desert.

She could feel his hand pushing the loose-necked dress off her shoulders, then his warm mouth was wandering the soft hollows and curves he had laid bare ... he was invading her privacy, seeing and handling her as no one had ever done. All the hopeless anguish she had felt in the desert swept over her again.

She writhed upon the cushions as the heat of his lips

pursued her, she pounded him and raked him with her nails, her throat stretched back to emit little gasps of appeal he ignored.

She felt lost under him ... he was wide in the shoulders, long in the legs, and her nostrils were filled with the mingled aromas of tobacco and leather, the tang of horses and his hot skin. His mouth was smoky as his teeth took hold of her lip and grazed the skin of her neck. One of his arms was bound around her like a bronze chain and she felt his other hand travelling the smooth surface of her leg.

Her body arched in a futile effort to throw him and she heard him laugh softly against her neck. 'I might take that for an invitation,' he said against her mouth. 'Shall I, *bint*?'

What he had already accomplished was enough of a violation, and Diane felt herself sinking beneath his kisses as she had sunk down in the sands, dazed, lost, the fight drained out of her.

'Enough!' His mouth dragged suddenly away from hers, and propped upon an elbow he gazed down at her face, his eyes half-closed, slumbrous between the thick lashes. Her resistance to him had tossed her hair into disarray and her lips still lay parted from the assault of his. The fingers of her right hand had locked themselves in his black hair as if trying to tug it from the roots.

'Stop trying to scalp me.' He jerked his head and her fingers loosened and slid down against his chest where his tunic had opened. The crisp hair grazed her fingertips and her eyes flew wide open, full upon his face only inches above hers.

'By the Prophet,' he murmured, 'to kiss lips which have never tasted the hot sweet wine of kissing!'

Diane lay supine in his arms, her lips aching and

aflame from their contact with his. She hated the fascina-
tion of his face and the intimate pressure of his body on
hers ... he made her feel so defenceless, so shamed and
furious as he slid his gaze down her figure. Abruptly he
drew himself away and lounged to his feet, a hand thrusting the black hair from his brow.

'Tidy your dress,' he ordered, turning his back on her
and reaching for one of his *cigarros*.

She obeyed him, adjusting the dress with hands that
shook. She glared at his averted back and would have
liked to plunge a knife between his shoulder-blades.

'I—I hate your guts,' she said furiously.

'Doubtless.' He shrugged his shoulders and smoke
eddied across to her. 'It's a natural reaction, but in time it
will pass. Be gratified that I am taking as much care to
break you in as I take with a spirited filly.'

'Thanks for nothing,' she retorted, smoothing her hair
with her hand. 'I've never been compared to a horse before.'

'Be flattered, *bint*. To an Arab a horse is the finest
creature Allah ever created; sleek, daring, fleet-footed.
The pleasure of riding across the sands on a fine mount
has little to compare with it.'

'Not even the distractions of your harem?' Diane asked
scornfully. She sat quiet now and her breathing had become more normal, even though she still distrusted him.

'Not even that,' he mocked. 'Did you imagine your
charms had risen to my head like a vintage wine?'

'No,' she said, 'only the desire to mortify me. That's
what you're out to take pleasure in, isn't it?'

'Exactly.' He swung to look at her, the *cigarro* locked
between his teeth as he regarded her. Then with a curt
inclination of his head he went out of the tent, taking
long strides and throwing the flap back in place behind

him. His smoke lingered, potent in her nostrils as the imprint of his mouth on hers. She sighed and a quiver ran all through her. She had to get away ... it had become imperative that Hiriz help her. Diane believed that the other girl would dare to do so; she hadn't liked it when the Sheik had ordered her to leave his tent. Diane thought again of that strange interlude with the sand diviner, but soon her mind was occupied again by the more realistic peril of her captivity.

The very idea of being taken by a man in order to slake his thirst for revenge made her crouch down among the divan cushions as if seeking a refuge.

Afterwards she would be but a thing to him ... she couldn't endure the thought and hoped wildly that Hiriz would be driven by jealousy to provide her with a horse. She had to escape from this place before the Sheik did more than press those burning kisses upon her lips ... his performance this evening had been but a rehearsal, a very deliberate one which had left her shaken to the core.

CHAPTER FIVE

By the leaping flames of the camp fires the Arabian girl danced. Tulle to her ankles hung from a beaded belt slung around the smooth curves of her hips. The small of her back and her belly were bare and glistening, and the gem in her navel winked like a wicked eye as she whirled and arched to the ground, tasselled bracelets sliding down her arms and tiny bells chiming about her ankles and keeping time to the pulsing, sensual music.

Suddenly the music paused and the dancer slid to the sand where the Sheik was seated, still moving her supple body to the beat of the drums. Diane, seated on the rug beside the Sheik, watched as he leaned forward and dropped a chain of glistening gold beads about the girl's bowed neck. Hiriz flung her black hair back from her face and stared intently at him. Her enormous eyes seemed to plead with him, and then with a brief laugh he tossed *kebab* into his mouth, crisply cooked on the steel points of swords which had been plunged into the glowing fires.

The pulsebeat of the music still throbbed in Diane's brain when she fell into bed. She didn't think she would sleep and was startled when she felt a hand shaking her awake. She sat up dazedly and saw a slim shape beside the bed, outlined by the oil lamp.

'It is I, Hiriz,' a voice breathed in Diane's ear. 'I have a horse outside and here is a robe and *sirwals* for you to wear.'

'It's still night time——' Diane shook the sleep out of her head and slid out of bed. 'Where is the Sheik?' she asked as she began to dress.

'Still asleep,' Hiriz replied, conjuring for Diane an image of him sprawled asleep in the bed Hiriz had vacated in order to come here with the clothing and the horse. 'Do be quick! I don't fancy his anger if he wakes up and finds me here—I have outside one of his best horses saddled for riding.'

'I don't know how to thank you,' Diane accepted the riding whip Hiriz held out to her. 'I know you're taking a risk and I—I'm terribly grateful.'

'If you ride away before we're discovered then I am thanked.' Hiriz swept her eyes up and down Diane in the *burnous* and Arab trousers. 'You look like a boy, so I presume you can ride like one.'

Diane nodded and clenched the whip. 'You remembered my water-bottle?'

'It's well filled. Come!' Hiriz had slit the rear wall of the tent with a knife and the two of them emerged stealthily into the dawn coolness where a long-limbed horse was tethered to a tent peg. Diane took firm hold of the reins and ignoring the sore stiffness of her ankle she climbed into the high-peaked saddle.

Hiriz untied the tether and stood there with her black hair flowing around her shoulders, reminding Diane again of the pagan abandonment of her dancing and the way her hands had beckoned the Sheik as she weaved her hips to the thudding of the drums and the wailing of the flutes.

'Ride quickly away,' she said, her eyes fixed darkly upon Diane. 'I hope we shall not meet again.'

'*Indeed!*' Diane dug her heels into the horse and as she felt the supple reaction of his muscles she realised that Hiriz had indeed given her one of the Sheik's best mounts. They galloped away from the goat-hair tents of the *douar*, the sands muffling the hoofbeats which seemed to keep time with the excited beating of Diane's heart.

As the encampment receded behind her she felt an exhilaration that cancelled out the worrying hours that lay ahead of her, when the sun would rise, the day grow hot and the sands stretch as if into infinity around her. She had an excellent horse under her and that, for now, was all that mattered. Her main purpose was to put as many miles as possible between herself and the Sheik Khasim who would be bound to come searching for her as soon as he discovered her absence.

Not, she reflected, out of any personal consideration for her but in order to stop her from reaching Dar-Arisi.

Diane had no intention of going to the police and creating a scandal, but the Sheik would assume so. All she wanted was to get word to her grandfather that she was on her way home to him ... she wanted above all to be safe with him again at their Breton house, and she relished the speed of the horse, with its proud head and long striding legs that carried her swiftly across the desert sands. With every passing moment they were turning from shades of lilac to a soft velvety gold. A breeze wafted through the folds of her robe and she breathed deeply as if laying up a store of fresh air before the sun burst into the sky and pervaded the atmosphere with dry heat.

Diane dreaded the sunrise, for then she would start to feel thirsty and her mount would begin to lose his freshness. She glanced around her and wondered how anyone could really love the desert. Its very vastness was an intimidation, yet her grandfather had revelled in its wild spaciousness, and to the man from whom she fled it presumably meant more than a woman ever could ... he had seemed when speaking of his harem to be dismissive, even faintly scornful of its attractions, but Diane had seen a different look in his eyes when he spoke of the desert.

To him it was more of a challenge, timeless and yet changeable, a slumbering tiger which might awake in a furious temper, or in a mood to be sublimely entertaining in its own untamed way.

Diane skimmed her eyes over the undulating golden landscape ... to her it was like a petrified ocean, indescribably awesome, giving rise here and there to great boulders polished by the sand grains shifting in the slightest breeze.

The sand flew from beneath the horse's hooves which touched the ground with spring-like movements. They passed a forbidding group of rocks where Diane felt sure she caught the movements of a prowling sand cat. A great bird hovered overhead, its wings spread dark as it prepared to swoop on the wild rock doves. Occasionally she saw a straggling patch of greenery or the pale gleam of animal bones, but not yet a track along which desert caravans made their way.

Its position would be marked by a man-made heap of stones, indicating that an oasis or a town lay somewhere along its route. Until she came upon such a sign Diane knew how vulnerable she was, how at the mercy of the desert ... and the man she hoped desperately to elude.

She had only to glance over her shoulder to imagine him in hot pursuit of her, the great blue cloak billowing around the savage grace of his body as he rode her down. She knew instinctively that he wouldn't spare his horse ... she had seen the spurs on the heels of his boots, an indication that he rode a powerful animal who was as tempered and wilful as he was himself.

Akin to the desert in every way, its moods and dangers strong in his veins. No woman alive could compete with all this, but he would pursue her because he craved the satisfaction of twisting a blade in her grandfather's heart. He had waited years to do it and unless she eluded him the Sheik would have his way. Yesterday he had only played with her, but if he ever had his arms around her again Diane knew she wouldn't leave them until he had stripped her bare of pride and virtue ... in her lay his vengeance because she was of value to Philippe Ronay, and once he discovered she was gone from the *douar* he would do his utmost to recover her.

A hunted look crept into Diane's eyes which were beginning to ache as the sun's radiance found and set shimmering the crystals in the sand. The pale salt beds were blinding, the very glare of them drying her lips so she had to reach for the water-bottle.

She took a sip and then gasped a protest at its nauseating taste ... water to which scented soap had been added in order to make it undrinkable!

Diane stared at the water-bottle, which Hiriz had assured her was well filled. She could hardly believe that anyone could be so cruel, least of all a mere girl. Diane felt deeply shocked, and scared. It might be hours before she came in sight of an oasis and here she was, alone in the desert with a bottle of soapy water and the acute memory of what it felt like to have a parched throat and blistered lips from a lack of moisture.

Anger shook her ... why had Hiriz played such a vindictive trick on her when last night the Sheik had favoured her with his company? After she had danced with him, he had said a brief goodnight to Diane and disappeared among the goat-hair tents with the other girl. Diane had assumed that he had gone with Hiriz to her tent, but now she wondered if he had extended that brief goodnight to the girl and left her alone as well.

With a sigh Diane hung the water-bottle on the saddle; she couldn't drink the stuff, but she could use it to moisten her skin, which would provide some kind of relief when she most needed it. The sun was smouldering overhead now and by noon it would resemble a molten flame in the sky when she and the horse would be forced to rest, preferably in the shade of one of the rock formations. While the sun was at its zenith the sand cats would wait until the cool of the evening to start hunting.

If only fate would be kind and lead her on to a caravan track, one along which camels had recently travelled so she would spot their droppings and the heart-shaped imprint of their pads. In the timeless desert the camel was used to carry goods as well as the chattels of nomadic families. The animal could survive longer than the motor engine, which if it couldn't be cooled down very soon burned itself out. The camel carried its own water supply and was almost impervious to the heat, a tough and resilient 'ship of the desert' swaying across the seas of sand, carrying cargo to the hidden cities which since Bible times had clung precariously to life amid a huddle of stone houses almost resembling ruins.

Diane had long been fascinated by her grandfather's tales of the desert, but it was only now that she understood its perils. She glanced about her as she rode and firmly held the reins of her mount. Above all she had to remain in control of the horse and her nerves. She couldn't afford to let either of them get the better of her ... she was at least free, no longer the prisoner of a man of merciless intentions. If she was going to perish in this godforsaken land then she would do it with dignity; her own person and not the possession of a man set on degrading her.

Again, driven by that innate fear of him that persistently nagged at her, Diane glanced over her shoulder but saw nothing that was living, only the limitless miles of sunlit sand patched in places by the towering rocks that the winds had eroded until some of them had the look of petrified giants. It wasn't a land meant for anyone to be alone in and she was grateful, at least, that she had the Arab horse for company.

She felt him supple and alive beneath her, but was

also aware that his speed had slackened and that he was starting to sweat. She slowed him down a little more; if he sweated too much he would want to drink, and he might very well turn in his tracks and head back for the *douar* if his drinking urge became too great. From the look of him he was obviously valuable, and Diane had learned from her grandfather that Arabs were clever at training their animals and this beauty might have been taught to find his way home, as the falcons and hawks were taught to respond to whistling signals.

'Take it easy for a while, boy.' She leaned forward and patted his neck. 'Soon we'll find a place to hide in, or we might be lucky and I'll spot a camel track——'

There Diane broke off and stared unbelievingly just ahead of her to where a neat pile of desert boulders had been stacked beside the unmistakable, beaten-down pathway along which animals and people had recently travelled. Some tin cans lay discarded there, along with a torn piece of donkey basket and a mount of droppings.

It was no mirage and Diane breathed a prayer of thanks to whoever had guided her this way. The track might not lead to Dar-Arisi, but it would certainly lead her out of the wilderness, away from the nightmare fear of being lost without any water to drink. She cantered the horse on to the track and smiled as he snuffed the air as if already he could smell an oasis or a town where he could dip his muzzle in a pail of oats. Diane had money in a small leather purse and felt confident she was going to make her way home to Brittany, taking with her some potent memories she wouldn't find easy to forget.

The track wove its way ahead of her, well trampled by what must have been a caravan of nomads who had obviously picnicked along the way and scattered the remains as they went. She was thankful for their untidiness, and instinctively glad that she hadn't actually met up with them. Even in a man like the Sheik Khasim ben Haran there was a primitive streak, so she could well imagine what untutored nomads were like; people who lived a wild and lawless existence in the desert. To them a girl like herself might represent sport or servitude, or even the dreaded danger of white slavery. In this part of the world, as she had so recently learned, a girl could vanish as if the sands had opened beneath her. If she was ever traced it would be to some den of iniquity on the Gulf, where she would be found steeped in drug addiction and vice.

Even in the heat of the down-beating sun Diane felt a chill of fear go sneaking through her body. She prodded her horse to a faster pace and he needed no urging, bounding along the track as in the distance a smudge of green and white showed itself against the skyline. Palm trees, habitations, someone in authority to whom she could go, her story already prepared in her mind. She had lost herself and some friendly Arabs had given her shelter and a horse; now she wished for transport to Dar-Arisi where she might pick up her luggage and sailing-ticket back to France.

Now it all seemed as simple as only hours ago it had been frightening; she had eluded the Sheik and could look forward to going home.

In the clear uncluttered atmosphere of the desert a town could seem within touching distance when in reality it was several miles away. It took Diane another hour of hard riding to reach the groves of trees on the outskirts of what she realised at once was a desert city.

The pungent scent of eucalyptus wafted from the deep green trees, while others had great drooping leaves and bulky trunks scaled like a crocodile's skin. Masses of them, forming arcades and colonnades around the towering walls of the city.

Diane cantered the horse along a shady lane among the trees, and the relief after the desert heat was wonderful. She took deep breaths of the dank cool air, for this vast area of trees made almost a jungle that teemed with smells and the sound of birds, and above all the dry grating chorus of the cigales. Fruits plopped down, rattling among the masses of leaves, and a jewel-plumaged bird flew from the path in a ray of sunlight.

'We've made it!' she exclaimed, sliding from the saddle and gathering the reins until the horse brought his head down against her. Diane stroked him, too accustomed to horses to be nervous of a pure bred Arab stallion. Arab men rarely castrated their male horses, as if it were an affront to masculine dignity, though when sold to the army the stallions underwent castration so they wouldn't fight each other.

'How, I wonder, do I return you to your master?' Diane ran a hand down the glossy neck. She supposed she would have to mention that the Beni-Haran had been her hosts and would ask that the stallion be returned to the Caid. Who was going to suspect, anyway, that a man with the title of Caid had threatened a European girl with rape? Diane shied away from the word ... she was safely out of his grasp and could forget the things he had said and the kisses he had forced upon her.

Forget? She led the horse out into the sunlight again, to where a great arching gateway led into the city itself. She found herself in an enormous market square, with long lines of stalls covered from the sun by plaited awnings that formed a continuous arcade. It was high noon and there were not many people about at the moment, only a few robed bundles taking their siesta in doorways.

The great square was cobbled like the walls all around it, and narrow alleyways led off from the market place.

Diane had to find someone who could tell her who was in authority here; she glanced around and saw a ragged boy scavenging among the discarded vegetables beneath one of the stalls. Diane took a coin from her purse and approached the boy, who glanced up when he caught the sound of hoof beats on the cobbled paving. He had huge dark eyes in an underfed face and when he saw Diane's eyes and the colour of her hair in the frame of the white *burnous* he backed away from her, clutching the cabbage stalks he had gathered.

'Don't be afraid.' Diane spoke in French, aware that some of these street urchins picked up a smattering of languages in order to beg among the tourists. 'I wish to pay you if you will show me the way to the house of the mayor—or perhaps I should say the Agha of your city. I need to speak with him. Look, boy, this money will buy you some dinner.'

The boy looked and his eyes glittered at the size of the coin on the palm of her hand. He reached out to grab it and Diane at once closed her fingers over it. 'Non.' She shook her head. 'When you have shown me the way to the Agha's house you may have the money—do you understand me?'

The boy studied her, eyeing her up and down as if uncertain of her gender. Diane smiled, aware of the oddity of her appearance in *sirwals* too baggy for her, over which hung the large *burnous*. Only her riding boots fitted her.

'Those cabbage stalks won't make a very good meal,' she said. 'I'm sure you'd like to earn the money for a good hot *couscous*.'

The boy glanced at the stalks in his hand, and then

disgustedly he tossed them away. 'Come!' He gestured Diane to follow him and she breathed a sigh of relief as she proceeded to do so, the reins of the horse wrapped firmly around her fingers. They crossed the square towards one of the arching alleyways and the glare of the noonday sun was muted as she followed the boy along the lane of flat-roofed houses and tiny shops like caves, among which hovered a smell of spicy food and coffee.

The boy turned and beckoned Diane to follow him around a corner, and here the medina opened out upon large houses, blank-walled at the front with archways leading into their crazy-paved fountain courts. Among them stood an ancient but still attractive mosque, its green dome standing among narrow fretted minarets, the walls of old-gold stonework set with oblong windows and doors. Palm trees shaded parts of the surrounding wall, etching fronded patterns against the sun-coloured stone. Seen at close quarters the doorways were sculptured into many strange designs. stone raised on stone to create an illusion of movement as shadows passed over them.

Diane felt as if all the old ways of the East were closing in on her as she and the boy went deeper into the network of streets, passing through a bazaar where during a busier part of the day she would have been beseiged by the sellers of copperware, leather goods. scents, silks and jewellery. But the time of siesta had fallen over the city and the owners of the shops wouldn't open up and reappear until the sun had cooled.

Suddenly she noticed that the bazaar wended its way beneath the high walls of an immense building, rambling on until a large gateway came into view, speared by points of iron along the top and with a Judas window let into it at eye level.

The boy paused there, his expectant eyes fixed upon Diane. 'House of Agha,' he said, indicating the formidable looking gateway.

The gate was firmly closed, but Diane just about managed to peer through the Judas window into a courtyard of palm trees and fountains. There didn't seem to be a soul about and she turned to the boy and asked if there was another way in. He shook his head, then gave a sudden grin and mimed with a bare and dirty foot the act of kicking. It didn't seem to Diane a very polite thing to do, to kick for attention at a stranger's gate, but it seemed about the only way she was going to get into the place. It was locked up like a fortress, no doubt to keep out the prowlers from the bazaar and the streets.

'Here goes!' She drew back a booted foot and aimed a kick at the gate. At once on the other side she heard a growl followed by a series of loud barkings; she had obviously aroused a guard dog, who from the sound of him would very soon arouse whoever was in charge of the gate.

'Merci.' She held out the coin to the boy, who took it eagerly, looked it over and then stowed it away in a pocket of his grubby *jellaba*. For today his dinner was secure and the smile he gave Diane was almost angelic; the next instant he was dashing away on skinny brown legs and she was left alone to await the opening of the gate.

It opened abruptly and a pair of tall robed men were standing there, one holding firmly the collar of a snarling dog almost the size of a donkey. Dark eyes raked her from head to toe, then one of the men took a good look at the horse, which had grown restive at sight of the dog and was pulling on the reins and scraping a hoof on the cobbled ground. The guard stepped forward and inspected the horse a little closer, then he flung some Arabic words over his shoulder.

'I wish to see the Agha,' Diane said in French, hopeful that if a street urchin had understood her request, then these men who actually worked for him would understand her. 'I need his assistance in getting to the town of Dar-Arisi, so could you please take me to him so I can speak to him personally.'

The tall guard frowned down at her, then he gestured at the horse and demanded in guttural French how she came by the animal. Diane at once told the story she had invented, that she had been lost in the desert and befriended by the Beni-Haran who had loaned her the horse. Put into words it sounded paper-thin, and right away the guard put his finger on its weakest spot. Why, he asked, had a member of the Beni-Haran not escorted her to Dar-Arisi? Was she unaware that she was many miles south of the place?

'I—I wish to speak with your employer,' she said nervously. 'Will you be good enough to take me to him— I'm European and I wish to go home.'

The guard with the dog then spoke in the Arabic that was lost on Diane. She felt tired after her long gallop and very thirsty; her ankle was throbbing and she flinched when the big dog bared its teeth at her. She was beginning to wonder if she had jumped out of the frying pan into the fire, for she was deep in the heart of a strange Eastern city, a lone girl accompanied by the thoroughbred horse no Arab would have loaned to a woman.

'You will come with us, *sitt*.'

Diane hesitated, and at once a brown hand reached for the reins of the horse and she was forced to follow him into the courtyard. The big gate closed behind her and she glanced quickly around and saw stone arcades leading into the interior and above them close-meshed wooden balconies that almost concealed the windows behind them. The place had a slumbrous, secretive look about it, and as she and the two men began to cross the courtyard Diane found herself counting the fountains that stood around it, some in sculptured stone, some in marble, and others whose basins overflowed with greenery and flowers instead of water.

There were exactly seven fountains in the courtyard of this rambling Eastern house and Diane felt a jolt of apprehension that made her stumble. 'The *sitt* is wearied.' A muscular hand caught and held her upright. 'You have been riding hard, eh?'

'I—I must see someone who can help me.' Diane looked up into the swarthy face of the guard and felt the pressure of his hard fingers right through the robe she wore. 'What is this place—is it owned by the Agha of this city? He's the man I wish to see.'

'The *sitt* will see him in due course.' The hand gripping her arm urged her towards the house. 'The Agha is not in residence right now, but as soon as he is a message will be given to him regarding your arrival. In the meantime you will be given food and drink, so come this way, *sitt*.'

Diane could do little else, the apprehension creeping through her body as the other guard took charge of the horse and led him away. She was led beneath a stone archway carved with Arabic script into a long cool hall of many arches and alcoves where rich-looking carpets lay on the mosaic tiled floor. There were divans in the alcoves and alongside them beaten-brass coffee tables or ones in carved wood. The arches were deeply incised to form a kind of filigree work and Moorish lamps hung here and there on long chains.

The sombre jewel colours and the glimmer of brass-ware should have had a soothing effect on Diane's nerves, but it was all so Oriental that it only increased her feeling that like a moth she had flown into a web of bewildering proportions. She had a sense of being helplessly stranded and half-dazed by the fatigue of her flight ... she had thought that nothing could be more nerve-racking than to be out in the open desert and surrounded for miles by nothing but sand and rock, but now it swept over her that she was all alone in a strange house, its alien scents in her nostrils, its high stone walls like those of a fortress.

She gripped the shaft of her riding whip as if she expected to defend herself with it. The guard swept aside a rich hanging into what she took to be a reception room, sparsely furnished with a divan, a table, and a window meshed in lacelike wood in place of glass. The Arab indicated that she be seated on the divan and she sat down on the very edge, still holding on grimly to her whip.

'Food and drink will be brought to you, *sitt.*' Curiosity glinted in the man's sloping eyes as they ran over the soft disarrangement of her hair; Diane gazed back at him with a defiant tilt to her chin.

'I am very thirsty,' she replied. 'I would appreciate something to drink—tell me, will the Agha be able to see me today?'

The guard spread his hands. 'We have word that he is arriving soon, but it's uncertain if he will be here today.'

'Oh dear——' Diane bit her lip. 'Is there anyone else I can see who might be able to help me? What I need is an escort to Dar-Arisi, so I can pick up my belongings at the hotel there and go on to the harbour. I really must sail home as soon as possible and I'm sure the Agha wouldn't mind if someone took me on to Dar-Arisi.'

'On the contrary, *sitt*, the Agha would be displeased if we allowed you to leave before he had a chance to speak with you. There is, you see, the matter of the horse.'

'But I told you,' Diane's eyes widened with a touch of alarm she was unable to conceal, 'I merely borrowed the animal and he has come to no harm. I'm quite a good rider——'

'The *sitt* would have to be,' the guard broke in drily. 'The animal is a full-blooded Arab stallion and there are few women who could handle such as he. Did the *sitt* notice that he bears a small brand on his haunches?'

'It's a Beni-Haran brand, I presume. I told you they were most—kind to me.'

'Permit me to say, *sitt*, that their kindness should have extended to an escort—the desert is a big place and you could easily have lost yourself.' The dark sloping eyes fixed their gaze on Diane. 'The brand borne by the horse is the mark that only the head of the tribe may use, so I feel it is best if you make your explanation to the Agha as to how you came to be riding such a valuable animal. In the meantime I will have a meal brought to you.'

'I didn't steal the horse,' Diane said, with a touch of anger. 'I want him returned to the Beni-Haran.'

'Rest assured he will be returned.' The guard withdrew from the room and the hanging settled into place over the entrance. Diane started to her feet as if to try and get out of this house, and then she subsided with a little groan as she realised how weary she felt. She needed to eat and rest and the sensible thing to do now was to accept the hospitality which had been offered her and hope that the master of the house would soon arrive home. He would then arrange for her to be on her way out of this country which had introduced her to one mishap after an-

other, and with a wince of pain she removed the boot
that was pressing against her sore ankle and massaged
the aching bones with her fingers.

What, she wondered idly, was the punishment for
horse stealing? She had heard that in certain parts of the
East a thief could expect to have a hand chopped off,
and she gave a shiver as she glanced around at the window whose meshwork gave her the feeling of being im-
prisoned. Her gaze moved to the doorway, and beyond
the sombre richness of the hanging she caught the
shuffling of a boot and realised indignantly that someone
had been stationed out there to make sure she didn't try
to leave.

She felt a burning sense of anger and injustice ... how
dared these people make a prisoner of her! When she
came face to face with the Agha she would have something to say about being taken for a horse thief. Damn
the Sheik Khasim ... it was his intolerable behaviour
which had led her into this present predicament, and
she hoped to heaven never to see his arrogant face ever
again.

Suddenly the hanging moved and a white-clad servant
entered the ante-room carrying a laden tray which he
brought to the divan table. The hand of another man
had held aside the hanging and Diane caught a glimpse
of dark robing such as the two guards at the gate had
worn.

The servant poured coffee for her from a long-spouted
pot, and uncovered the food dishes containing fried liver
and kidney and various vegetables. '*Merci*,' she nodded
at the servant, who salaamed and withdrew. Diane
sipped the coffee thirstily, and proceeded to eat the meal
with resentful eyes upon the doorway. It was a wonder
these suspicious people hadn't given her bread and water

instead of a lunch which she grudgingly admitted was well cooked and enjoyable. Her dessert was rice pudding flavoured with a dash of cinnamon and slices of apricot. She ate every morsel and drank some more coffee, and feeling a lift to her spirits went across to the wood-meshed window to see which part of this enormous house it overlooked.

Diane saw a stone courtyard absolutely rampant with foliage and wall vines studded with flowers, clambering everywhere in a riot of gold and red and deep purple. Bougainvillaea, she realised, and sheets of jasmine and roses. Oh, how she would enjoy sitting out there rather than being confined to this sombre little room!

She approached the doorway and drew aside the hanging. Immediately the Arab who stood there swung to face her ... Diane thought she was going to faint as her gaze rested on the scar deeply embedded in the tanned skin of the lean and haughty face. Her hand clenched the material of the hanging for something to hold on to.

'You!' Her heart beat heavily with a recognition of fate—danger—a sense of doom.

'None other, *mademoiselle*.' He gave her an ironic look and watched as she backed into the room as if trying to get away from his tall figure in the big dark cloak cascading around him from his throat to his leather kneeboots. He followed her with the noiseless tread of a tiger, those eyes of his, so unforgettably *yeux de feu*, were fixed upon her shocked face.

'I waited until you finished your lunch, Diane. I didn't wish to take away your appetite.'

'W-what are you doing here?' she gasped. 'Did the people here send for you——?'

'My dear girl, I live here.'

'What do you mean? I—I was told the Agha lived here!'

'So he does.' The Sheik swept a lean hand from the ropes of his headwear down past his scar to the folds of his cloak. 'He stands before you, Diane. Haven't you realised that the horse being one of mine brought you to Shemara——'

'Oh no!' Diane's legs wouldn't support her and she fell down weakly on to the divan; somewhere deep inside her the suspicion had stirred when she had counted those seven fountains in the courtyard, yet still she gazed unbelievingly at the tall figure of the man she had tried so desperately to escape. Instead of eluding him she had walked through the gates of his *kasbah*.

'But for the intelligence of Rumh you could have found yourself in grave danger,' he said grimly. 'It would seem, however, that in your eyes I represent more danger than the desert.'

'Yes——' The word was barely audible and she couldn't take her eyes from the savage gold of his skin against the black material of his cloak, his eyebrows slanting black above his angry eyes and proud arching nose. The tip of her tongue edged itself around her lips. 'What are you going to do with me, treat me as a horse stealer?'

'A good hiding might be a good idea,' he glanced significantly at the braided whip in his hand. 'Are you going to tell me who helped you to get away from the *douar*, or do I make a guess?'

'I—I saw the horse in the camp's compound and helped myself——'

'Little liar,' he said bitingly. 'The horses are valuable and a close watch is kept on them; only someone I trusted could have provided you with Rumh, which is our word for a lance. Appropriate, eh? The animal rides

straight and swift, but he's strong. You are a more pro-
ficient horsewoman than I realised.'

'I expect you've examined him from head to fetlocks
in order to make sure I haven't damaged him,' she said.

'Assuredly, but you've been well taught and had you
misused a thoroughbred like Rumh he would have
thrown you by rearing on his hindlegs and tossing you
from the saddle, easy enough for a strong horse with a
woman on his back.'

'It would seem, Sheik Khasim, that men and horses
alike are trained to your orders. I had been told that a
powerful chief has a long arm, and I imagine you are
laughing up your sleeve because I still haven't managed
to get away from you—damn you!'

'I'm glad to see your spirit isn't crushed.' A smile
curled about his lips. 'It's one of the things I admire
about you, Diane, and doubtless my admiration incited
Hiriz to assist you in your bid for liberty. You were a
trifle unwise to trust her, she has a penchant for playing
tricks on people that aren't always amusing.'

'She gave me a water-bottle filled with soapy water,'
Diane said, a rueful look in her eyes as they met his. 'I
was hardly amused when I took a sip of that!'

'Yes, I think that young woman needs to be turned
over a firm knee. I shall have to arrange it.'

'She won't enjoy chastisement after being such a pet
at your knee, but I suppose you think women enjoy your
slap as much as your tickle?'

'Quite.' His eyes held Diane's, glittering dark steel that
pinned her where she sat. 'You seemed to enjoy the
dancing last night—you may recall that during the performance one of my men came and spoke to me. He had
just ridden into camp from Dar-Arisi.'

He paused, watchfully, and Diane felt herself holding
her breath. Then in mute appeal she held out a hand to

him as if begging to hear what more he had to say—she sensed that it was significant and could feel her heart pounding.

'I should have spoken with you last night, Diane.'

'You had something else on your mind! Oh, what is it? Is it something about my grandfather?'

'Why do you say that?' His voice was low-pitched, his gaze holding hers relentlessly.

'Because I feel it—because I have to get home to him and you have to let me go!'

'I have this to tell you, Diane.' His hand moved and closed firmly upon her shoulder, as if he braced her body to take the shock of bad news. 'I was informed last night that a message had been received at your hotel requesting that you return home. Philippe Ronay suffered a stroke and was taken to a Breton hospital where he passed away without regaining his senses. I fear you won't see him again, Diane. Ronay has gone to his rest.'

Diane swayed and the next instant was caught against the Sheik's great cloak, an arm enclosing her while his free hand swept caressingly over her hair. She accepted this in a kind of apathetic daze, too wounded for the moment to give way to tears or anger. It hammered in her brain that instead of telling her about Grandpère last night he had set it aside because his pleasure with his dancing girl came first. 'It's true?' she whispered.

'Unfortunately for you, yes.'

'You—you wanted to torture him—he's dead because of you!' Suddenly dumb shock had given way to a painful, driving need to hurt this man whose vital aliveness was pressed so close to her. As if her fingers had a will of their own they found the knife at his hip and pulled it swiftly from its sheath ... the next instant she slashed at him, feeling the blade rip his clothing and enter his flesh. He swore as he pulled away from her; the knife slid from Diane's fingers as she watched him clutch his side and find blood on his hand.

'By the Prophet!' He caught his lip between his teeth. 'Has doing that made you feel better?'

'I hope it's made you feel worse.' Diane was trembling. 'Your devilry has killed Grandpère—you had your way a-and paid him back, didn't you?'

'Did I, Diane?' The Sheik winced and pressed his cloak tight against his side; blood was seeping through the material and Diane watched it as if hypnotised.

'Oh—damn you! I hope it hurts like hell!' She clenched her hands and pressed her lips against her knuckles, shivers of reaction going up and down her spine until she could have screamed.

'I assure you it hurts.' The Sheik watched her in silence for a tense moment. 'The news regarding your grandfather was received at your hotel soon after you rode to the old fortress in the desert where he was stationed long ago. You and I, Diane, didn't meet until much later that day, and by then he was already out of reach of my retribution. He died peacefully, but I have no desire to join him. Come, I have to get this injury attended to before I delight you by dying in front of you.'

'Some hope of that!' she said huskily. 'It would take more than a gash in the side to kill a devil like you!'

'So you feel no stab of compunction?' he drawled. 'What is making you tremble—fear of what I shall do to you?'

'Nothing you do could hurt me any more,' she said tonelessly. 'You must be feeling very disappointed now my grandfather is out of your reach.'

'He might be, but you aren't.'

'You can't mean to keep me here? There's no more reason——' She broke off as his eyes filled with silent taunting amusement.

'How ineffably innocent you are in so many ways,' he mocked. 'Have you forgotten we have a saying, *mektub*, which in your language means what is to be will be.'

Diane stared at him and the thudding of her heart seemed to fill her ears so she couldn't think straight. She shook her head. 'No—I have to go home. There's no one else. I'm all he had.'

'Of course, Diane. His sole relative a granddaughter who has vanished in the desert. Come, be resigned to the inevitable, *ma chérie*.'

'Don't you dare to call me *darling*!' A sudden blaze lit her blue eyes and she attempted to dash past him, hoping the stab wound had slowed down his reflexes. It hadn't, and she cried out as his hand flashed out and caught her in a vice-like grip so that when she struggled his fingers felt as if they might break her bones.

'I won't be treated like this——' She struck at him wildly and he raised his voice and called out for one of his men. Instantly the door hanging was swept aside and Diane felt herself taken hold of as if she were a doll and lifted off her feet in the huge hands of a man whose skin was as sable as his robes were white.

'Take her to the harem,' the Sheik ordered. 'This one is a wildcat who has to be taught how to be a woman. Place her in the custody of Lalla Hathaya, and ensure that she can't get her hands on anything with a cutting edge.'

'You brute—you son of a devil! You can't do this to me——' But it was happening, and all the Sheik did as she was borne away by the powerful Moor was to smile briefly, a hand pressed to his injured side.

'You wait,' Diane shrieked as she was carried along a corridor into the interior of the *kasbah*, 'I'll get you in the heart next time!'

'Be quiet!' The Moor shook her as if she were made of rags. 'No woman speaks to the Caid of Shemara like that!'

'Don't you mean the Cad of Shemara?' Suddenly the delayed misery swept over her and she was sobbing like a child when the Moor carried her across an enclosed courtyard where the twisted limbs of fig trees cast shadows on the surface of a pool and where wall lanterns in wrought iron showed the shapes of lotus trees hung with plum-like fruits. An atmosphere of intrigue and mystery pervaded this place, where a great arched door was almost hidden by a mass of bougainvillaea.

It was opened and Diane was carried across the threshold . . . a captive in Sheik Khasim's harem.

CHAPTER SIX

THE room was large and sumptuous, the soft light of Moorish lamps glimmering over the carved cedarwood, the mellow carpets, the ceiling of lustrous tiles laid in patterns. Diane stirred and opened her eyes, still languid from the long sleep which had overtaken her after being given a drink which had probably contained a soporific to calm her nerves.

She lay there on the big square bed, overcome by a feeling of unreality, as if she were awake in a dream. Her gaze wandered up the swathings of filmy muslin about the bed . . . like a web, she thought drowsily, in which she was ensnared and could not at the moment struggle against.

From the oil-holders of the copper lamps there stole

an aromatic scent and the gem-light gleamed on the tables and chests with their tracings of silver marquetry. Ibises and falcons flew on painted wings across the panels of the walls and because there was no sound of a clock ticking in the room Diane had no way of guessing how many hours had passed since she had been brought here in tears.

The tears had long since died away, but not her feeling of desolation; her terror-edged sadness that she would never see her grandfather again. Now there was no one to care what became of her. She had vanished in the desert, and after a while she would be listed as officially missing and if a search for her had been organised it would be called off soon and the authorities at Dar-Arisi would shrug her off as a foolish young woman who had ventured into the Sahara and come to grief through her own lack of common sense. They knew what a vast and mysterious place the desert was; a region of nomadic wanderers and hidden cities, and that searching for a girl in such an area would be like hunting for a needle in the sand.

Her gaze wandered across to the *mesharabiya* that covered the windows with its delicate carving. Beyond the meshwork lay a velvety darkness, and as she grew less languid and more curious she finally sat up and found that she was clad in a sleeping garment of incredibly fine silk; the very sheets she lay upon were fine and silky and the bedspread itself was as gorgeous as the spread-out fan of a peacock.

'Take her to the harem,' the Sheik had ordered, and here she was, in the very heart of the *kasbah*, surrounded by the sensuous luxury of one of the apartments where his *kadines* were kept.

Diane sat there wondering what was going to happen

to her, the beats of her heart filling her eardrums until suddenly there came the sound of a key grating in the lock of the arched door. As the door widened so did her eyes until the doorway was filled with a tall figure in a white silk tunic casually open to his belt. He stood animal still, but Diane felt an erratic throb of the heart.

When he moved inside the room and closed the door behind him, she involuntarily crouched back against the pillows and suffered the play of his eyes over her. Smoke drifted lazily from the *cigarro* clenched between his teeth as he took her in, slender and lost-looking beneath the canopy of the big bed.

'Do you feel rested?' he asked. 'You have had a long sleep, eh?' Now the *cigarro* hung from his fingers and suddenly within the shadow of his lashes his eyes were like black flame. Lamps glowed upon the walls near where he stood and cast their gem-light over his features; he looked strong and sure in his power over her: he knew as she knew that he could have her at his will ... that was why she had been brought here, her clothes removed and taken away, replaced by a slip of silk that barely concealed her from his gaze.

'How long have I slept?' Her hand clenched the silken coverlet and drew it towards her; she wanted to snatch it around her and hide from him.

'Almost from the moment you were brought here,' he replied, 'and that was yesterday evening.'

'Who put me to bed?' she asked, her body tingling from his look.

'It wasn't I, regrettably.' A smile came and went at the edge of his mouth. 'I was in the hands of the *hakim* being sewn up. Aren't you going to ask if I'm feeling better after such a blood-letting?'

'I can see what kind of health you're in,' she retorted.

'You're as fit as one of your own stallions.'

'Thank you for the charming interest in my wellbeing, Diane.' He bowed his head mockingly. 'You look in excellent shape yourself, *ma belle*.'

The tingle ignited into a burning, all-over blush and as she hastily wrapped herself in the bedspread a soft laugh issued from his lips. 'That is like trying to call off the hawk once it has seen the dove,' he mocked.

'With all your women,' she retorted, 'I shouldn't think one more comes as any great surprise.'

'Ah, but there is always an element of curiosity in the possession of a new toy.'

'I'm not a toy—and I'm certainly not your possession!' She said it fiercely, with more spirit than conviction.

'Don't delude yourself, Diane.' He lifted his *cigarro* and drew on it. 'You are as much mine as a dove taken in the desert by my hawk. I choose to have you, and who is there in all the world to come and claim you from me? To those beyond the walls of Shemara you are a headstrong girl who rode into the desert never to be seen again. To those within the city you are the private concern of its Caid, and here in the East, *chérie*, a man in my position has authority over everyone who resides within his territorial jurisdiction.

'Apart from which,' he smiled as he regarded the room, sweeping his eyes around it and resettling his gaze on her, 'a woman is a man's private business in this part of the world, so resign yourself to your situation. It isn't so terrible, is it? You have been given every luxury, and if you behave yourself I shall allow you to become acquainted with Shemara itself. You will find it a fascinating place.'

'How can a prison be fascinating?' She looked at him with tormented eyes, for it seemed as if nothing could be worse than having her freedom taken from her by an

Arabian autocrat to whom women were amusing toys of pleasure.

'If you choose to regard the *kasbah* as a prison, Diane, then it will feel like one. It would be wiser to think of it as your home——'

'My home is in Brittany!' she exclaimed. 'What sort of man are you that you can audaciously tell me that I must regard this—this harem as my home? I'm not a girl of the East. I haven't been brought up to be a man's *toy*!'

'My dear child,' he approached a sofa table and stubbed out his *cigarro* in an ashtray, 'the almighty Allah intended just that, that a woman should be a creature who pleases the eye, the touch, and the senses. Why else would he have made her so silken-skinned, so shapely, so melting to the masculine hand?'

'He intended people to—to love one another——'

'Then by all means let me love you.' He began to approach the bed, treading the carpets noiselessly, gradually looming over her until Diane was conscious of little else but his lean face, his eyes within their shadowing lashes, the bronzed strength of his torso where the white silk lay open to the leather belt.

'Come, my bit of sugar, be as sweet as you look.' He reached down and his fingers gripped the bedspread she held around her. As he took hold of the coverlet and pulled it out of her grasp, Diane scrambled from the bed and fled from him across the room. She was so anxious to get away from him that she didn't notice the big floor cushion that lay in her path and she had stumbled over it and fallen to the floor before she could save herself.

In just a couple of long strides the Sheik reached her and before she could regain her feet he was kneeling over her sprawled figure and holding her supine with mercilessly strong hands. Diane gazed up at him, lost for breath and with terror welling into her eyes. His pupils had dilated and his nostrils flared in time with his breathing ... his hands tightened and he drew her slender, struggling, lightly clad body up against his bare chest. Diane gasped as she felt his hardness against her softness.

'Oh no—please!' she gasped huskily.

'Don't be afraid, *chérie*.' He gazed down at her and she saw the excitement smouldering in his dark eyes, flickers of flame in their Arabian density ... like the desert at night. 'I have no intention of hurting someone so sweet and slim. I shall lead you carefully to the door of pleasure before I carry you across the threshold.'

Even as he spoke he rose to his feet and lifted her with him ... Diane felt the rippling of his muscles, and then she was being carried back to the bed, waves of chill and flame sweeping over her, making her almost too weak to go on resisting him.

'Come,' he laughed softly, and swept the hair out of her eyes, 'when I want a woman I don't allow her timidity to stand in my way. You have such blue eyes, Diane, such a silky bow of a mouth——' He brought his lips down close to hers and gave a sigh that wafted his breath over her face. It was warm, smoky, slightly minty, and his firm teeth glimmered between his parted lips. Diane lay there as if transfixed, and then she felt him arching her body against his and even as she tried to turn her face aside his mouth covered hers.

She had expected demand and aggression, but he took her lips in a succession of kisses, holding, teasing, running like flame over the sensitive surfaces of her mouth. Kisses that induced in her a strange kind of helplessness, as if she were falling into a whirlpool, as if she were spinning through spaces of sensation, with nothing to cling to but the hard maleness that felt so alive and warm.

He drew a little away and she sensed that he was studying her face ... she forced her eyes to open and her languid gaze was filled with his face, as frightening to her as it was fascinating. Close to him like this she could have fitted her fingertips into the scar that long ago had slashed open his cheek to the bone. Curiously enough it didn't make him ugly but somehow intensified his look of strength and assurance.

'Does my scar repulse you?' he asked.

She was going to say that it didn't, but she needed a defence against him. 'It doesn't exactly enhance your looks, does it?' she said. 'It sets the seal on your position, I imagine. People expect a tyrant to be fierce-looking, don't they?'

'So in your eyes, Diane, I am a tyrant?'

'I'm quite sure, Sheik Khasim, that you follow the principle that you should dominate and other people should accept your domination. You've already intimated that as an Arab leader you have a lot of power.'

'Quite so, *bint*, I have power, but don't accuse me of misusing it.' His jaw went suddenly hard and before she could attempt an evasion his mouth had taken hers with aggression. She was borne back against the pillows and his body was heavy upon hers, pinning her down, a hard knee forcing its way between her legs. As she felt this happening a jabbing fear of the outcome swept through her, but her attempts at resistance only seemed to bring out the savagery in him.

'Don't call a man a tyrant and expect him to behave like a gentleman.' He gave a laugh that rasped against her straining neck. 'You haven't yet learned, my innocent, that flattery will soften a man but defiance will only harden him.'

'Flatter you—*you?*' She pummelled him with her fist,

aware with a heart-thudding desperation that he was at the very gates of her innocence. 'You're cruel—outrageous—nothing but a barbarian! I—I'd like to see you in hell!'

'First it will be in paradise, *ma belle*. Now lie still or I shall hurt you more than need be——'

Her desperation came to a peak and remembering where he was vulnerable she brought her own knee slamming in against his side. 'Ah!' The cry was wrenched from him and Diane felt the shudders of pain go through him. 'Ah, you wildcat—by Allah!'

He took a ragged breath and slowly sat up; Diane saw that he had gone ashen around the lips and nostrils, making his features look even more chiselled. He put a hand inside his shirt and felt himself, wincing again with pain. Diane watched him, the pulse thudding in her neck; she had reacted not really with the intention of hurting him so badly but from the instinct to protect herself. Now she realised that she might have opened the knife wound and made him bleed again.

'Is it bleeding?' She spoke huskily from a dry throat.

'Inevitably.' He sat there looking at her from beneath black forbidding brows. 'You intend to fight me to the bitter end, don't you, Diane?'

'If I have to,' she admitted. 'If I hurt you then you asked for it.'

'Presumably.' His gaze drifted down her figure, to where the night slip was in disarray around her slender legs. He reached forward and closed his fingers around one of her slender ankles. 'Most women in my life have been bought with kisses and trinkets, but you are not of their sort, are you? What do I give you, eh? Moon diamonds? Rubies? Your own Arab horse? There has to be something you want that will permit me to have you in my arms without risking some form of injury. I tell you, if another woman put her knee into me I'd take my whip to her.'

'I'm surprised you hesitate in my case,' Diane rejoined.

'This white skin of yours would show the marks too vividly.' His hand moved along the slim calf of her leg. 'What do I give you to make you pliable?'

'My freedom,' she said, her fingers gripping the bedcovers, her lips tense around the words, her heart beating madly inside her.

'*Diable!*' He surged to his feet and stood glowering down at her. 'That is the one thing I refuse to give you.'

'Why?' She sat up, her eyes wide with pleading. 'Does having me here to torment mean so much to you? You can't hurt my grandfather any more, and you know that I'll never stop hating you.'

'Won't you?' A faint smile curled itself around his lips. 'You look maddeningly attractive when you hate a man, *chérie*. Why not love me instead and then I might grow bored with the usual submissiveness; the willingness to please me because I happen to be the Caid. There, I give you a choice, Diane. Fall in love with me and I'll let you go.'

She stared up at him, her eyes intensely blue in her white face. 'I could never find it in me to love you,' she said bitterly. 'You have no compassion or sympathy in you—you're an Arab!'

'Yes,' he quietly agreed. 'And in your eyes that makes me a barbarian, especially when I lay my hand upon you and you see the difference in the colour of our skins. Did Ronay teach you that to be white is to be a superior person? Did he impress upon you that Arabs are primitive tent dwellers whose women are fit only to be used, or struck down by sharp steel running with blood? If we are a hard and suspicious nation, *bint*, it's because we have been well taught by our desert and by those who have tried to conquer us that trust and love make weak fools of those who open their hearts to it. Our needs are akin to the desert of which we are a part; we are bred to combat its dangers, and our passions are a match for its flaming sun. We can't afford to be soft, but our pride and our lineage is a match for anything the French can boast of.'

His words seemed to touch a flame to Diane's skin; it swept over her, for she hadn't meant to imply that as an Arab he was beneath her for being a European.

'I—I didn't mean that——' She bit her lip and glanced down to where his lean dark hand lay against the slim pallor of her leg; his fingers moved against her skin and sent a quiver through her body.

'You are a sentimental child who thinks love is an emotion rather than a hunger.' He leant down abruptly and the warmth of his lips crushed hers and then slowly released them. '*Ma fille*, you will learn and I intend to teach you the lessons you so obviously need. It will, I am sure, prove an enlightening experience for both of us. In the process you may discover that our culture and our way of life is as interesting as your Anglo-French up-bringing has been.'

'Then,' Diane slowly raised a hand to the lips he had kissed, leaving upon them a lingering sensation she wanted to erase, 'then you intend to keep me here?'

'Yes, aren't you flattered when there are other women in my house who are only too pleased to have my company?'

'They're welcome to your company,' she said stormily. 'They're here because they want to be, but I'm your—prisoner!'

'Agreed, fair one.' He smiled in that brief way and ran a hand over her hair. 'In the old days of the more ruthless pashas a woman with your skin and hair would have been worth a high price in jewels and spices. The Barbary pirates used to ransack the seas for your sort of woman, rare in the harems where most of the occupants were brunette.'

'Don't touch me!' Diane pulled away from his touch. 'You're no better than a Barbary pirate yourself and you're educated enough to know it, which makes you that bit worse! There will be a search party out after me, so what will you do if they come to Shemara making enquiries? I was seen riding into Shemara—a boy brought me to the *kasbah*, a little ragged boy who is bound to remember that I gave him some money.'

'If he was a ragged child then he was a nomad,' the Sheik said a trifle curtly. 'Those people come and go and will be miles away by now. A tyrant I might seem to you, Diane, but I don't allow in my city the kind of poverty that might be seen elsewhere. We have schools for the children and care for those who are parentless.'

'I'm parentless,' she broke in, 'but you care little about me. All I am to you is a—a body!'

'Are you?' He laughed softly and swept his eyes over her. 'Most of my men would regard you as far too slim to have much appeal to the sensuality. They could hardly refer to you as "my moon", could they? Unless they were thinking of moonlight when it glows soft and silvery across the desert sands at night.'

'How poetic,' Diane scoffed. 'Am I supposed to feel complimented?'

'Don't you?' His eyes held glimmers of amusement deep inside their darkness. 'Be honest, Diane, or are you still such a child that you aren't fully aware of how appealing you are? It's a practice in the harems to give a woman an appropriate name when she enters, and I think I shall refer to you as Opal, with your combination of white skin, gold hair and blue eyes. You see, I don't think of you as only a body. There are many lusher bodies than yours in Shemara.'

'Like so many Oriental carpets,' she rejoined, 'all laid out for your lordly comfort? Opal, indeed. I have a perfectly good name and I prefer to keep it, thank you!'

He stood regarding her, black-haired, lean and scarred, his chest deeply bronzed in contrast to the loosely worn tunic and dark *sirwals* that somehow intensified his agile look. The edge of his mouth quirked as he selected a brown-leafed *cigarro* from a leather case, making the leaf crackle in his fingers before applying a flame to it. The strong smoke drifted towards Diane and his silent scrutiny induced in her a nervousness she couldn't completely hide. To the bottom of her spine she was aware of his vigorous maleness combined with a strong will and the power to command.

'If you could see your eyes,' he murmured. 'Your mother was English, eh?'

'It's no business of yours what my mother was! She didn't have me for your sort of purpose—oh, how I hate it here!' Diane twisted her hands together and looked around her in a hunted way.

His eyes followed hers around the large room, with its arching windows covered in a lacelike tracery of wood, reaching from ceiling to floor where cushions were heaped for reclining on. Rugs and brasses hung upon the walls, and beneath crescents of shelves stood bridal chests ornamented with Oriental designs. Everything was as alien to Diane as he was.

'You need have no fear of being confined here,' he said almost casually. 'You ride well, Diane, so you will be allowed to ride in the desert with me.'

'If I'm a good girl, I suppose, and bow down to your dictates?' Yet at his words her heart had leapt with excitement at the prospect of riding in the desert without the constant fear of being lost there.

'Yes, you like that idea, don't you?' He captured her gaze and held it searchingly. 'But don't imagine you'll be given the chance to elude me, I'm an Arab and I can always ride you down, but I have a feeling there is much for you to enjoy in the desert; the golden spaciousness, hills and valleys that hide strange communities, the utter stillness of dawn, and the colours that spill over the dunes when the sun sets and a mantle of shadows bring mystery to the night. When night advances across the desert a strange luminosity comes with it, brought by the stars that seem closer to us, almost to be touched from the great dunes that rise to meet them. Yes, I think you could find an affinity with all that, eh, Diane?'

'I don't doubt that the desert can be fascinating,' she said offhandedly, 'for someone who doesn't have to regard herself as a—a prisoner.'

'My prisoner of love?' he mocked, sprawling down upon a fleece-covered divan and lifting long legs upon it, the toe of a black slipper pressing into a cushion. 'In the heart of all women there is a fear of love and a desire for it.'

'Love,' she exclaimed, 'bears no resemblance to—to what you have in mind.'

'And what do I have in mind, *chérie*, apart from providing my prisoner with every kind of comfort?'

'I don't need to spell it out, do I, Sheik Khasim?' There was something so intimate about the way he sprawled on the divan, smoking his *cigarro*, and watching her through those sensuously dark lashes. To Diane who had known only the companionship of an elderly soldier, in many ways wrapped up in the past, he was a disturbance and yet at the same time her only protection in this Arab city so many miles from the sound of sea-birds flying over the Breton coast, and the voices of French people in the shops and in their gardens where they clipped their raspberries and hung out sheets to dry in the salty air.

'One would think,' he drawled, 'that I was a bloated pasha, smoking a hookah and dribbling sherbet all over my hennaed beard. Do I seem so monstrous to you?'

'I regard your behaviour as monstrous, and women judge men by the way they're treated by them,' she said spiritedly.

'Has it occurred to you, Diane, that had you fallen into the hands of nomads you would have been treated to a dirty sack on the bare floor, a tin plate of mutton stew once a day, a beating from the women if you didn't do as you were told, and no doubt attentions from the men that would have been far less refined than the attentions you have, according to you, suffered at my hands—which are washed regularly?'

Diane gave a shiver she couldn't control; she knew that what the Sheik outlined could well have happened to her, and there was certainly no denying that he was a scrupulously clean man, down to the very fingertips of his lean muscular hands.

'As we say in the desert, Diane, you must look at the Sphinx from both angles; there may be shadows on one side, but examine the other profile and you will see the sunlight.'

'That's all very well,' she argued, 'but when I came to see the Sahara I didn't come with the intention of staying here. Brittany is my homeland and I—I love it.'

'What is love?' he murmured through the updrifting

smoke of his *cigarro*, his eyes narrowed and thoughtful. 'The reflection of oneself as in a pool one sees in a mirage. It seems to be there, a tangible oasis one could arrive at, but it's only a dream that vanishes in the blinking of an eye. Brittany was your home, Diane, but now Shemara takes its place and you will learn to adapt to your new environment.'

'But why?' she demanded, kneeling up on the bed and holding out her hands to him in a gesture of supplication she was hardly aware of. The silk transparency of the night slip clung around her in fragile folds, and her hair was endearingly tousled around the charm of her face, her lips half-open, pleading like a child for something she was being unfairly denied.

He watched her, intent and still as a tiger whose prey was only a few feet away. 'That, *chérie*, is the most foolish question you ever asked anyone.' His smile was at its most subtle. 'You know why, so don't suddenly play the innocent, as if I have taken you from a nunnery where you believed the wind and the water gave birth to the birds and the fishes. You are a woman, I am a man, *n'est-ce pas?*'

She flushed slowly but wouldn't cower away from those demanding eyes, where deep at the dark centres of them a flame seemed to beckon and burn. 'The desert has made you a cruel taskmaster,' she said. 'When you want something you have no scruples about taking it, have you? My feelings mean absolutely nothing to you and I—I have to live with that, so you say!'

'So I ordain,' he said arrogantly. 'Like all women you start quibbling when you get nervous.'

'Like all men you are glued to your own wants and opinions,' she retorted. 'Don't you care that I hate you?'

'Hate, like love, is a tree with many branches.'

'You Arabs must have as many proverbs as you have sand in the desert.'

'Yes, we are rather fond of quoting them, and like most adages they have a basis of truth to them. People are fond of saying they hate something, or they love it. What they really mean is that something deeply disturbs and excites them and that if it was suddenly missing from their life they would fall into a state of apathy or despair.'

'Are you saying, Sheik Khasim, that if I were missing from your *kasbah* you would feel like that—you with all your lush and obliging women?'

He gazed across at her, a slim and kneeling figure framed by the fine saffron netting and overhead the delphinium-blue tiles with motifs of birds, crescents and flowers. He seemed about to say something when all at once the door of the apartment was thrust open and a woman appeared in the arched aperture.

Diane turned a startled head and at first glance she took the woman for one of the Sheik's *kadines*. She was dusky-skinned and draped in an almond-green robe worn over *sirwals* of emerald silk. Jewels sparkled in her ears, and it was when Diane looked into the dark eyes set within clustering lashes that she knew who confronted her ... this was Morgana, the Sheik's sister.

'Well,' he drawled, rising to his feet, 'couldn't you contain your curiosity a moment longer, dear sister, and had to come and see the new addition to the household?'

'So this is she?' Morgana sauntered into the room, perhaps two or three years younger than her brother and equally striking to look at. She paused at the foot of the bed and surveyed Diane from the crown of her fair head down to her slim bare feet.

'I see you have the girl where you want her, brother dear,' she drawled.

He raised an eyebrow at his sister, then looked at Diane. 'This sister of mine has something in common with you, Diane, a dash of pepper on her tongue. She persuaded me a year or two ago that I should allow her to see Paris, Rome and Venice and she picked up the European tendency to be flippant, but apart from that she is nice enough. I should like you two to become friends.'

'Does the girl need a friend, Khasim, when she has my big virile brother to keep her company?' Morgana slowly smiled, but Diane caught a gleam of mischief behind her long lashes and realised that the Sheik's sister was ready to be friendly with her.

Their eyes met and Diane wondered what Morgana thought of her brother for keeping a European girl locked up in his house ... did she approve of such behaviour and despite her travels regard him as a law unto himself?

Morgana strolled across to her brother, her almond-green silks floating attractively about her slim figure. Reaching up to him on her toes she slid an arm about his neck and murmured something in his ear. He listened, dark head bent to her, then Diane saw a rather startled look come into his eyes ... eyes that dwelt upon herself before he drew away from Morgana and strode to the door.

'I will leave the two of you to become acquainted.' He stood a moment in the doorway, a reflective look in his eyes as he absently fingered his scar. 'Please refrain, Diane, from petitioning my sister to provide you with a horse so you can gallop off into the desert once more. I have warned you of its dangers and I assure you, you are much safer here at the *kasbah*.'

'That's according to your definition of safe,' she rejoined.

'*Touché*.' He inclined his head and a smile lit his eyes deep down. 'At least for now you can regard yourself as safe, eh?' The door closed behind his tallness, and with a low-pitched laugh Morgana curled herself down on the divan he had vacated.

'Are you afraid of my brother?' she asked.

'I have reason to be, wouldn't you agree?' Diane sagged among the pillows where the Sheik had held her in his powerful arms and taught her how fragile were female defences ... how like an uncontrolled flame were male passions when aroused.

'I had heard that the Ronays had courage.' Morgana watched Diane through a cloud of dark lashes. 'Or is it only my brother the Caid who can make Diane Ronay tremble?'

'So you know who I am?' Diane felt humiliated, as he had meant her to feel. Clad like a slave, kept under lock and key, the symbolic price always paid by the captured woman of an enemy.

'You possess a dangerous name.' The jewelled hoops glinted in Morgana's earlobes as she studied Diane. 'My brother is very proud and he doesn't forgive easily those who have hurt him.'

'I've never hurt——' Guilt stabbed at her, for she had put a knife into him. 'He has no right to keep me here—you know he hasn't!'

'You prefer it in the desert to being looked after in my brother's house?'

'You're twisting things so he's in the right and I— I seem a fool.'

Morgana shrugged. 'He's the Caid and even I, his sister, am as much under his sway as anyone else in Shemara. During my travels I saw that European women had much more freedom than we women of the East and for a while I became rebellious of Khasim's control over my life. There was a young man with whom I became infatuated and I wrote and told my brother that I wished to marry this boy. Within hours an emissary was sent from Shemara to fetch me home. I could have killed Khasim at the time, but later on I realised that he had done the wise thing and saved me from making a fool of myself. He knew that I was too young to know my own mind.'

'You are his sister,' Diane pointed out, 'but I'm an Anglo-French citizen who is being held here against my will. He may have a kind of parental control over you, but in my case he hasn't!'

'I don't imagine he would want that kind of control over you.' Morgana smiled and studied a bangle on her wrist. 'I wonder, Diane Ronay, if deep in your heart you truly wish to leave him. He has great charm when he cares to exert it.'

'I assure you I'm immune to his—charm.' Diane spoke with passionate conviction. 'I've no wish to stay segregated like one of his harem women!'

'The harem is occupied by relatives. Upon occasion my brother has been presented with girls by other Sheiks and as diplomatically as possible has arranged for them to marry his officers or various cousins. As to a collection of them here at the *kasbah*,' Morgana gave an amused laugh, 'believe me, it is only a rumour, because few people from outside ever enter these premises. Bear him in mind, Diane. Does he look the type of man who indulges in debauchery? Whatever his faults, and I admit

he has a certain amount of self-will, he isn't a sensualist
who thinks of little else but his appetites. He's a man of
the desert who likes to ride and hawk with the Beni-
Haran tribesmen, that is when he isn't listening to peti-
tions or passing judgments on tribal offenders.'

Morgana paused and her eyes dwelt with sudden
seriousness upon Diane. 'He has his work cut out, you
realise, being head man of a tribe which is so large that
sections of it extend into the far reaches of the southern
desert, where there are large encampments of Beni-Haran
people, guardians of immense sheep and goat herds, not
to mention the thoroughbred horses which are bought
by racing men all over the world. Khasim could, like
other sheiks of great power, be a man of the world who
travels as his own diplomat for the concerns of his
people, but he adores the desert too much. It is the
desert—so far—which provides my brother with his
pleasure and consolation when he has attended to the
concerns of his tribe.'

Diane had listened to his sister in a fascinated silence
... she allowed her imagination to dwell upon his hard,
well-exercised physique; upon his bronzed features and
keen eyes. In his desert robes he had a hard-striding look
of command ... no, he wasn't a sensualist, but why—
why did he insist on keeping her a prisoner in his harem
when he wasn't basically a man who indulged in sexual
licence?

'If your brother isn't truly a cruel man, then why does
he shut me up like this?' Diane drew a sigh. 'My grandfather is dead. He has paid the price for those lost lives in
the desert long ago. What more does Sheik Khasim want?'

'You.' Morgana said it almost inaudibly, as if not to
startle Diane. 'You must know what lies behind his con-

finement of you. If he can't have you willingly, then he will have you unwillingly.'

'And you condone his action?' Diane said incredulously. 'I am to be his toy and no one in this house will raise a hand to stop him?'

'He's the master——'

'You're an educated woman, Morgana, and yet you bow down to his will and think that I should. Does nothing change in the East where women are concerned? Are they still—slaves?'

'In a number of ways,' Morgana admitted. 'Perhaps because there is something deep inside a woman that responds to male domination. I will tell you something, Diane. Arab men don't take for granted the differences between the sexes. They don't regard a woman as equal for the simple reason that they are too conscious of her "magical powers". Oh yes, a woman can make a son for an Arab and, believe me, that makes her important in a way that European men don't appreciate. A woman can soothe his aches and cares, and then give him pleasure in his manhood. While in France I envied women who had your kind of freedom, but after I was brought back to Shemara I realised that I wanted the protectiveness I had under my brother's wing. The dove and the hawk is the symbol of our house, did you know it?'

Diane shook her head. 'Don't your wings ever ache for flight?' she asked. 'Do you ever go riding in the desert?'

'When I am in the mood.' Morgana stretched her bangled arms lazily. 'I am soon to be married. I will then leave Shemara to go and live in Casablanca with my husband. He will reside there as official diplomat for the Beni-Haran. His name is Rauf Al Ahmar, and my brother has allowed me to meet and speak with him—he's very attractive.'

'Do you love him?' Diane asked curiously. 'Is he your choice, or has your brother chosen him for you?'

'He's attractive to me and so I shall learn to love him,' Morgana replied. 'It was at Khasim's suggestion that I became acquainted with Rauf. I abide by my brother's decision that it's a good match. My hand was asked by a prince, and strictly speaking as sister of Khasim ben Haran I should make a rich marriage in my own class, but Rauf is thirty-five and this other man is in his sixties. Khasim refused the alliance on my behalf and I am indebted to him. I shouldn't wish to be the bride of a man old enough to be my father, but it happens. Khasim has seen to it that I have a husband of virility to hold me in his arms.'

'But wouldn't you prefer a romantic courtship, Morgana? It hardly seems right to me that your brother should do the choosing for you, though it's obviously part of his nature to presume that he knows best!'

'I expect our ways seem strange to you, Diane, but had I not found Rauf to my liking, then Khasim wouldn't insist that I become his wife. Rauf is strong and good-looking; a fearless desert man like my brother. I think, Diane, that you take too seriously the idea that a man and a woman should be madly in love before they decide to marry. Love can blind us to the faults we would otherwise notice, and a woman besotted with love might fail to realise that the man she loves is cruel or selfish and she then has to suffer for it.'

'Be that as it may,' Diane argued, 'everyone is entitled to make their own emotional mistakes, and I still consider it high-handed of a brother to take charge of a sister's—love life.'

'It's our way of life and we don't question it.' A smile flitted across Morgana's face as she regarded Diane's look of seriousness. 'Arab men are the masters of the home and they believe that women need protecting from themselves. They take the view that if a man and a woman are left alone together the man will make advances which the woman would be too physically fragile to reject. It's taken into account in the East that everyone has sensuality in them and so young people are guarded against bringing dishonour upon themselves and their parents.'

'You say all that, Morgana, yet you condone your brother's behaviour with regard to me!' Diane looked indignant. 'Is it all right for him to—dishonour me because I don't happen to be an Arabian girl?'

'He's the Caid of Shemara——'

'That hardly excuses him! If a man carried you off, Morgana, and shut you up in his house with the intention of toying with you, then you know very well that your brother would hunt him down and whip the hide off him. I—I have no brother to defend me. I have no one!'

'That isn't so,' Morgana murmured softly. 'You have Khasim.'

Diane gazed at the Sheik's sister in a kind of stunned wonderment ... Morgana couldn't possibly mean what she had just said. 'He—he's the very man I need protection against!'

'If you fight him,' Morgana agreed. 'Hasn't it entered your head, Diane, that it might be more pleasant for you if you didn't fight him?'

'No!' Diane swept a hand down her figure in the silk night slip. 'How can you think it right that he should treat me like this? How do you think I feel—it's humiliating!'

'Some girls might consider it flattering.' Morgana nibbled the tip of a finger. 'My brother isn't just any man, is he? His title in England is equivalent to that of a lord.'

'And that gives him the right to keep me here—like this?'

Morgana merely smiled in answer and it swept over Diane that she couldn't expect any kind of help from her. As far as Morgana was concerned her brother's commands were law ... his desires above judgment. It was there in her Arabian eyes what she was thinking ... Diane would be made to give in to Khasim ben Haran and she might as well surrender gracefully.

'I shan't—I'd sooner die than belong to him,' Diane said passionately. 'I know in my bones what he wants— he wants to crush my pride and then he'll toss me aside like a piece of trash! He'll never forgive me for being part of Philippe Ronay and he won't be satisfied until he can send me away from Shemara without anything left in my soul except shame. Can't you see, Morgana, he has to do that so he can put his own ghosts to rest? I—I'm his scapegoat.'

'My brother has never hurt a woman in his life——'

'No woman of your race, but I'm different, and where I'm concerned he's pitiless. I—I've been alone with him, Morgana. I know his intentions. He has to hurt me so he'll be rid of those boyhood images that haunt him— I see it in his eyes when he looks at me—I feel it in his hands when he touches me—I hear it in his voice when he speaks to me!' Diane's own voice held a broken, husky note. 'He's a full-blooded Arab and he believes it was meant to be that I should come to the desert and that he should find me. I don't think I shall ever forget the look on his face when he realised who I was. For him it has to be ... he has me in his snare a-and when I think of him my heart goes crazy, as if it's a bird trying to get out of a cage.'

The two girls gazed silently at each other here in this beautiful jewel-lit room, deep in the heart of the *kasbah*, the Sheik's fortified palace set within high walls beyond which teemed a maze of alleys where cage-like balconies hung from the walls of the crowded houses. There in the night flutes and drums pulsed to a strange sensual music and right now a dancer in black gauze might be arching her body like a bow, her gold bracelets sliding down her supplicating wrists as she laid herself at the feet of the Sheik.

Shemara seemed to Diane a barbaric place where anything was possible. If the police or the army came searching for her, they wouldn't be allowed inside the harem of a powerful Arab. No one from the outside world would be allowed to enter this secluded section of Khasim ben Haran's house ... she was indeed a captive dove in the hawk's cage.

CHAPTER SEVEN

'No!' Morgana broke the silence with a cry of protest. 'No, Diane, you have misread my brother's intentions.'

'I think not.' Diane huddled down on the bed. 'I'm the granddaughter of his bitterest enemy and where I'm concerned there's no mercy in him, least of all the indulgence I've seen him show towards Arab women. He can't forget that one of my grandfather's soldiers hacked your mother to death and he—he needs the catharsis of making me

suffer for all that carnage. Just to think of it terrifies me!
I've only to look at him and I see what he wants burning in his eyes!'

Diane buried her face in her hands as if to try and blot
out the images the Sheik evoked in her mind ... the dark,
black-lashed eyes burning into hers, threatening her as he
loomed over her, powerful and potent with the sensual
dangers her sheltered way of life had not prepared her
for.

'Perhaps you think Khasim cruel because he's an Arab,'
said Morgana.

'I think I bring out the cruelty in him,' Diane replied.
'Whenever he comes near me I feel a—a sort of violence
in him. When he touches me I feel almost a pain, as if a
whiplash passes over my skin.'

'He bruises you?' Morgana looked incredulous as her
eyes swept over Diane, probing her skin for any telltale
marks of bruising.

'Inwardly,' Diane murmured. 'It's a sensation inside
me rather than an outward wounding that leaves its
mark.'

'His effect on you seems very strong.' Morgana tin-
kered with a charm on one of her bangles, a little
diamond horn that glinted. 'Surely you realise that my
brother is an unusual Arab. I have heard him remark that
certain rulings in the Koran are hard on human nature,
that for instance a man and woman should make their
ablutions after they have made love. I don't think this
the attitude of a hard-natured man.'

'I'm sure he's very passionate——' Diane looked away
from Morgana in a confusion she couldn't hide; she felt
sure that he had long since broken the Koranic rule his
sister had just mentioned. Somehow she couldn't imagine
him living, or loving, by any rules except those of his

own making. 'Do you never oppose his wishes, Morgana? What if your arranged marriage fails?'

Morgana shrugged her shoulders. 'Casablanca is a large, interesting city and there are smart dress shops and restaurants there. As a married woman I shall have more freedom to make friends outside the home and if marriage disappoints me I shall find other compensations. Even Arab women do so. It isn't the prerogative of Europeans, you know.'

'Where has all the romance gone?' Diane said a little cynically.

'Perhaps to be too romantic makes a woman too vulnerable—like you, Diane. You are a romantic, eh?'

'I suppose I am.' A wistful smile flitted across Diane's face. 'I don't think I could accept your kind of marriage, or your philosophy that there are compensations in smart dress shops and, presumably, flirtations with passing strangers. I believe for me it would have to be life or death.'

'That is very extreme, *chérie*.' Morgana broke into a laugh. 'Don't you find it at all romantic being locked up in the harem of a real live Sheik?'

'I consider it outrageous—it's no laughing matter, Morgana! His Arab ways are natural to you, but try putting yourself in my shoes.'

'Ah, but you aren't wearing any.' Morgana stood up from the divan and came across the room to Diane, dusky-eyed, her hair flowing darkly over the almond silk of her tunic. 'You and I could have fun, you know, if you will only try to enjoy living here at the *kasbah*.'

'How can you speak to me of enjoying myself——?'

'You are *très charmante*,' Morgana ran her eyes over Diane, 'and my brother is in private a rather lonely man. I think he may have discovered a need for a woman's companionship, and he can be kind in his own way.'

'If I'm willing to become his slave—to take his orders and bow down to him until I've no will of my own!' Diane shook her head fiercely. 'There is only one thing I want from him and it's something he'll deny me to the bitter end—I want my release! You call him lonely? I call him arrogant!'

'No doubt, but all in all a man, and a woman belongs in the arms of a man.'

'Any man but him!' Diane's eyes were a stormy dark blue. 'He's shut me up so he can tame me—my clothes have vanished and I've nothing to wear but this slip of a thing!'

'The question of clothing can soon be settled,' Morgana smiled. 'I have cupboards of dresses and we seem to be of a similar size. You are welcome to come to my apartment and choose whatever appeals to you.'

'That's kind of you,' Diane ran her glance over the Arabian draperies Morgana was wearing at the moment, 'but I don't really feel at ease in Eastern clothes.'

'I have French and English fashions in my cupboards, so don't worry about that.' Morgana ran considering eyes over Diane. 'Personally speaking I imagine that our soft styles would suit you, but you may take your choice of whatever I have. Khasim is a generous brother and I spend much of my allowance on the latest styles. I think we shall be friends, don't you, Diane Ronay?'

'Don't you bear me a grudge for being a Ronay?' Diane gazed rather wistfully at the Sheik's sister and thought again how strikingly alike they were about the eyes. The likeness seemed to end there, for Morgana seemed a much more sympathetic person.

'I was too young at the time to fully realise what had occurred, but Khasim remembers more vividly because he was there when the encampment was destroyed and he bears on his face the mark of the sabre that struck him and almost killed him. I was here at Shemara in the care of a nursemaid—ah, it was all very terrible, Diane, but none of your doing.'

'I wish your brother would be so reasonable,' Diane sighed. 'That's why my clothes have been taken away so I'm made to feel at his mercy. I know he wants to wring every scrap of vengeance out of me, the last of the Ronays, and then he'll toss me aside like a bone he has picked clean.'

'I'm sure you exaggerate——' Morgana looked troubled, despite her remark.

'No——' Diane shook her head and gave a sudden shiver as a cold breeze threaded its way through the meshwork of the windows. 'His face was like iron when he told me that my grandfather had died. Grandpère was dear to me and always kind, and I can only judge him as I knew him—can't I?'

'Khasim judges the Colonel as he knew him—come, Diane,' Morgana caught her by the hand, 'come to my apartment and select some dresses for yourself. I have clothes galore! You will see!'

Diane was pulled off the bed, hurried out of the room and along a corridor they were about to turn when a tall figure came striding around it, a riding cloak enclosing him from throat to heels. He paused abruptly and Diane felt confusion sweep over her, for to see him clad for going out while she was en déshabille made her want to curl up in a blushing heap.

'Running away?' he demanded.

'Diane needs something to wear and we're going to sort through my cupboards for some suitable dresses,' Morgana told him. 'Where are you going, Khasim?'

'I'm dining out with a friend.' Abruptly, however, he unbuckled his cloak and to Diane's surprise he swept it around her figure, enclosing her completely in its rich warmth. He gazed down at her startled face, running his eyes over her flushed skin to her half-parted lips. He seemed to lean down nearer as if to take her lips and Diane instinctively shrank away from him. At once a mocking glint came into his eyes.

'My riding cloak has never looked so picturesque as it looks on you, *ma fille*. You should have your portrait painted in it.'

Diane didn't know how to reply to him; for once she was lost for words: he looked picturesque himself in a superb kaftan, tight-legged *sirwals*, and headrobes bound with double cords in which gold threads glinted. He looked every inch the Arab lord, the headwear intensifying the autocracy of his lean scarred face.

'Go with my sister,' he said abruptly. 'As fetching as you look right now you can't run around my house like that. I'm sure Morgana will be able to provide you with everything you need.'

'For how long, Sheik Khasim?' Diane spoke huskily, a curiously tight feeling in her throat.

'For as long as it takes, Diane. Go and enjoy yourself. *Leyltak sayeedah!*' He strode off with the words and left her standing there in his cloak, gazing along the corridor to where he had vanished from sight but not from her mind, filled with a vivid image of him in his Arab regalia. His looks and his voice seemed imprinted upon her senses and suddenly her knees were shaking beneath her. She felt as if she might faint, and when Morgana spoke her voice seemed to come from a distance. It took quite an effort for Diane to pull herself together, her be-musement not altogether dispersed when she found her-self led into a room so cluttered with furniture, ornaments, silk screens and lamps that it resembled a bazaar rather than a bedroom.

There was barely space to walk between the items of furniture to where tall carved cupboards filled an entire wall. Morgana opened them and Diane caught her breath in amazement when she saw the collection of clothes inside, bulging together on hangers, in all shades of the rainbow, in all sorts of styles and materials.

'There you are,' Morgana flung a handful of dresses down on one of the divans, 'take your choice!'

'I've never seen so many dresses,' Diane fingered the georgette skirt of a turquoise creation. 'How do you manage to wear them all?'

'I just like to have them.' Morgana smiled at Diane's wide-eyed look. 'I adore pretty clothes—don't you?'

'I've never really thought about it. Back home in Brittany with my grandfather I wore shirts and breeches most of the time, or shorts when I went down on the beach. We rarely went to parties, so I didn't feel the need for more than a couple of long dresses.'

'You had only two formals?' Morgana looked astounded. 'I can't resist the feel of silk and chiffon against my skin and I love buying perfumes in the market place. You must come with me one day! I go to an old man there who mixes the most subtle aromas which are distilled into quaint little bottles. I shall ask Khasim to let you come with me into the *kissaria*. I've known the place since I was a small girl and I still find it fascinating, as you will, Diane.'

'I—I doubt if I'll be allowed to come with you—your brother knows I shall run away from him the first chance that comes my way.'

'Not with his Moorish guards treading upon our heels,' Morgana laughed.

'You mean you aren't allowed out on your own?'

'Not even when I visit friends. Whenever I go beyond the gates of the *kasbah* I am followed by an attendant. I am the Caid's sister and there is always the chance that I could be abducted, either for money or by one of the political factions out for trouble.'

'The kind of trouble my abduction can't cause, is that it?' Diane murmured, her fingers clenching the soft georgette. 'I can vanish, but nobody gets concerned, least of all the Caid.'

'Diane——' at once a look of contrition sprang into Morgana's eyes, 'I didn't mean to sound as if you are unimportant. I—I suppose I don't think of you as having been forcibly abducted by Khasim. After all, he didn't throw a sack over your head and gallop off with you across his saddle-bow.'

'No, but from the moment he found out who I was he set out to humiliate me. I've never met anyone so high-handed—striding about in his great cloak like some lord of the earth!'

'He is a lord of the desert, so it comes naturally to him to be like that.' Morgana studied Diane in her brother's cloak, a deep blue against the fairness of her hair and the pale gold of her neck. 'I'm used to Khasim as a brother, but I suppose he must seem intimidating to other women. Poor Diane! Is he the first man to—well, you know, make you afraid for your innocence?'

Nerves quivered sensitively deep inside Diane at the very thought of what close proximity to the Sheik did to her ... fear, turmoil, panic, turning her into a stranger to herself. The very folds of his cloak around her was an intimate reminder of his arms holding her close, then closer to his powerful body, warm and vibrant and most definitely a threat to her innocence. Every look and word they exchanged was charged with his need to cauterise his wounds in the white-hot flames of a passion that made Diane tighten his cloak around her, shielding her body in the very warmth that caused a fevered chill to sweep through her veins and hammer at her temples.

'I—I suppose my grandfather looked upon me as the next best thing to a boy,' she said breathlessly.

'But Khasim doesn't look upon you in that way, eh?'

A quivering sigh escaped Diane and she gazed rather helplessly at the pile of colourful dresses on the divan. 'Haven't you something more simple for me to wear?' she asked tentatively.

'I have no breeches and shirts to offer you—now let me see.' Morgana rummaged through her cupboards and withdrew a pale cashmere garment, unembellished except for the slits at each side of the hem. The cashmere was soft and creamy to the touch.

'It feels nice,' Diane murmured. 'I think it is more my style, don't you?'

'It's a *jellaba*,' Morgana smiled, 'but I do agree that it's elegant. Do you want to put it on now?'

'Please,' Diane spoke fervently, 'but I shall need some underthings——'

'Select whatever you like.' Morgana swung open a drawer layered with satin and *crêpe de chine* lingerie which had the look of Paris about it. 'Come, take an armful, Diane, while I find you some more *jellabas*, then you will feel less like a harem slave, eh?'

Diane smiled herself as she selected several pairs of glossy French knickers and matching slips, rich with lace at the hems. Morgana certainly believed in pampering herself, or so it seemed to Diane, who had always worn simple white underwear. She discarded the big cloak, folding it and laying it across a leather stool, and then as if it still projected too much of the owner's personality she turned her back on the cloak as she quickly dressed in the garments Morgana had been kind enough to give her.

'Turn around!' She was studied from every angle by the Arabian girl. 'H'm, you need some. beads to add colour, and slippers. What size are you?'

'A narrow fitting four——'

'Then we can complete your *ensemble*.' Morgana produced a pair of embroidered slippers and a chain of opals, and a minute later Diane was standing there looking strangely charming in the *jellaba* with opals at the neck, long full sleeves, the narrow skirt reaching to her ankles where the side slits revealed her slim legs.

'A bracelet as well,' Morgana decided, and clasped around Diane's left wrist a wide silver one embossed with Oriental patterns. 'There! Look in the mirror at yourself, Diane! You're beautiful!'

Diane gazed in the cheval glass at a figure she barely recognised. The cashmere clung softly to her contours and the opals threw out blue lights that matched her eyes. Opal! That was the name the Sheik had mockingly said he would bestow on her as a member of his harem ... except that he didn't possess any such thing but allowed the harem quarters to be used by relatives.

Her lips moved in a tentative smile as she smoothed her hair. 'I wonder what Grandpère would have said if he could have seen me dressed like this?'

'Like an Arab girl?' Morgana quirked a slender eyebrow and instantly her resemblance to her brother sprang vividly to life. 'You stare at me, Diane.'

'You are at times so like the Sheik. It's in the eyes—you both have such dark irises and such thick lashes.'

'We resemble our mother. Come with me, Diane. I should like you to see the portrait of her which our father had painted soon after they were married. She wears her wedding outfit in the painting, similar to the one I shall wear when I marry Rauf.'

'I've seen the man you're going to marry,' Diane said impulsively. 'He was at the Sheik's *douar*—he was the man your brother sent to Dar-Arisi to find out if I was travelling alone and he—he came back with the news that my grandfather had died and that I was to return to Brittany. All of you seem to fall in with the Sheik's wishes even when you know them not to be fair. Has your fiancé reason to hate me for being a Ronay?'

'Both his parents were killed in the raid—oh, I don't know what to think.' Morgana caught at Diane's wrist, the one that bore her bracelet with the little jade monkey attached. 'I don't know if it's right or wrong for people to cling to old grudges, even those steeped in the blood of loved ones. I don't believe it's revenge that my brother wants—not in his heart. It may even be that for once in his life he's unsure.'

'The Sheik *unsure*?' Diane gave a laugh that wasn't too sure of itself. 'He has to satisfy his Arab sense of justice.'

'Our mother came from Kurdistan, did you know that?' Morgana fingered the jade monkey. 'She was among a batch of girls who were being sold—yes, Diane, you look at me wide-eyed, but even to this day it happens in the far reaches of the Sahara where the laws as you know them just don't exist. Had you fallen into nomadic hands it could well have happened that you were put up for auction as our mother was. Word reached our father that one of the girls was particularly lovely and he provided the money so she wouldn't be bought as a slave. She discovered that her benefactor was the Caid of Shemara, so she came to thank him, and they fell in love and he took her for his one and only wife. After her death he never remarried—come with me and I'll show you what she looked like. You might understand once you've seen her why Khasim finds it hard to forgive the cruel way she died. He was thirteen and old enough to realise that she and our father had found a special kind of love—perhaps that romantic love that even death can't destroy.'

Morgana led Diane from the harem quarters into another section of the rambling *kasbah*, with its odd flights of stairs leading from one floor to another, and its dim cool rooms where every sound was magnified. She noticed that an attendant followed them at a discreet distance, walking silently and clad in white but for a red cummerbund in which a knife was sheathed.

'This place is positively turn-of-the-century,' she murmured. 'How do you stand it, Morgana?'

'I expect Selim has orders to watch you,' Morgana rejoined, with a smile. 'So will it be each time Khasim is absent from the house; one of his trusted guards will watch you vigilantly in case you persuade someone else to let you have a horse so you can lose yourself in the desert, or be carried off by mercenary nomads not above selling a blonde virgin in the market place. I expect that girl Hiriz hoped you'd fall into such hands, but she keeps most of her wits in her feet and chose for you a horse specially trained by Khasim. He has a way with animals and is a trained vet, did you know?'

'He certainly has a way with dancing girls. I saw Hiriz dance for him at the *douar*. She's exceedingly pretty and very jealous of any attention he gives to other women.'

'Yes, she has sharp claws,' Morgana agreed. 'She was given to Khasim when she was thirteen years old——'

'You can't be serious!' Diane came to a standstill on

the stairway down which they were walking and gave Morgana a disbelieving look. 'You mean she really is a slave girl?'

'Yes, Hiriz belongs to him and he can do with her exactly as he pleases. Are you shocked, Diane?'

'It seems so barbaric——' Diane bit her lip and lowered her eyes. 'No wonder she was so jealous because I was at the *douar* and installed in his tent. I suppose he turned her out while I was there——'

'Khasim doesn't live with her!'

'I thought——'

Morgana shrugged her shoulders. 'She's just a kind of pet he dallies with, no more than an amusing doll he indulges when he's in the mood. Hiriz would love to marry him, of course, for there's power in being the bride of the Caid of Shemara, but my brother would require more from a wife than a facility for dancing to the desert drums.'

'Will he punish Hiriz do you think?'

'Would you like him to do so?' Morgana gave Diane an intent look.

Diane shook her head. 'I'm not vindictive, and she's very young. I was a fool to imagine she really wanted to help me.'

'She wanted you out of the way because she saw at once that you have something to offer which she lacks——'

'I'm offering nothing,' Diane protested. 'And as far as looks are concerned Hiriz is stunning, far prettier than I could ever hope to be.'

'Pretty like a doll,' Morgana said scornfully. 'When she isn't dancing she is just an inane little chatterer. I beg of you not to wish her upon me as a sister-in-law— not that I've many fears upon that score. I have an idea

Khasim will marry her off to one of his officers——'

'But he——' Diane broke off and looked away from Morgana.

'You were about to say something about my brother, Diane?'

'I was informed that he only gives virgin brides to his men.' A flush stung Diane's face; the words had been strangely hard to say.

'So he does.'

Diane stared at the wall beside the stairway, and then she looked at the Sheik's sister. 'I—I suppose I took it for granted that Hiriz was his *kadine*.'

'I would suggest, Diane, that you never take for granted anything to do with my brother. He's an unpredictable man in lots of ways, and though many Arab men would have made use of Hiriz from the moment of her presentation, Khasim has not treated her in that way. He had her taught dancing; he enjoys very much watching our kind of dancing, that of the woman entertaining the man to music. He isn't addicted to your own kind, Diane, though I rather enjoy it myself. My brother is very much of the desert, akin to its fierceness and much of its loneliness. Were he not the Caid he would, I know, be happy to live there as the Bedouin live, his home a goat-hair tent that can be rolled up and placed on the back of a camel, owning a few animals and free to explore the great golden spaces of the Sahara. That would be his wish, but instead he has the care and protection of the Beni-Haran in his keeping, and a self-centred creature such as Hiriz is unsuited to be his consort.'

'If he finds her distracting, then what more could he want? If Arabs consider that they know better than a woman, then surely they don't require intelligence in a wife?'

'You know very well, Diane, that my brother is no ordinary man.'

'He certainly has more than his share of lordly assumption,' Diane agreed. 'I—I thought that he and Hiriz looked very suited to each other. Surely he must find it very flattering to have someone so devoted to him?'

'His hawks and horses are also devoted to him,' said Morgana. 'So you thought Hiriz was my brother's *kadine*, eh?'

'It's none of my business what she is to him.'

'No?' Morgana tilted an eyebrow and slowly smiled. 'Then it didn't trouble you to think of Khasim making love to Hiriz in the tent to which he took you?'

'I'm sure I couldn't care if he has made love to a thousand women.' Tilting her chin, Diane descended the stairs to a great hall of palm-shaped columns and stonework rich with blue and topaz tiles. The soaring columns made her feel rather lost as she walked among them with Morgana ... lost in time and miles removed from the quiet uneventful life she had led until the urge to visit the East had become too strong to resist.

She looked about her with half-frightened eyes ... a place of looming shadows cast by great lamps on chains, of arched doors, and a blaze of Oriental imagery in the stonework and woodcarvings of the hall. She also noticed the guards who stood silently here and there, and was conscious of the curiosity in their eyes as she walked past them with the Sheik's sister.

Morgana paused in front of an arching door and beckoned the attendant Selim to her. Diane gave him a rather resentful look as Morgana spoke to him in Arabic; did the staff of this household regard her as the Caïd's *kadine*, his woman to be watched night and day ... as if she were of personal value to him? As Diane well knew her only value to Khasim ben Haran lay in revenge and she was to sweeten the bitterness he refused to bury with the woman whose portrait she was about to be shown.

Selim entered the salon and lit the lamps, which smoked a little on their copper bases as he replaced the tinted shades. The room was large and cold in the way of a room not often used. Underfoot was a wonderful carpet of a thousand mixed colours; overhead the ceiling was a honeycombed tracery of gold-coloured wood, and the Oriental furniture had a silky patina, black almost as ebony, centred by a crescent-shaped divan heaped with cushions in sombre silks.

The effect upon Diane was of a gloomy grandeur, as if not for a long time had people gathered here to be sociable and to enjoy the beauty and comfort of the room.

It was, Diane decided, a place of memories, and she watched Morgana lift one of the lamps and carry it across the room, where she paused and played the light over an immense painting that hung against the panelled wall. Diane approached and stood beside Morgana and together they gazed up at the woman in the canvas.

There in the dark, beautiful eyes lay the same ineffable smile Diane had seen in the Sheik's eyes, but where distinction was at war in his face with a deep strain of ruthlessness, the face of his Kurdistan mother was utterly calm and lovely. A shimmering ankle-length veil was elegantly draped about a lovely, very simple silk dress, its sheen as subtle as moonlight. A silver girdle embraced her slim waist, and the border of each hanging sleeve of the dress was exquisitely embroidered in silver. The fine soft glow of her skin was enhanced by the silk dress, and a necklace of heart-shaped rubies and diamonds was her only ornament.

The frame of the portrait had a lotus-blossom design all around it, and underneath there was some Arabian script.

'What do the words say?' Diane asked.

' *"In life you can have only one great love."* ' Morgana turned to look at Diane. 'The lotus-blossom carving is our symbol of eternal youth. It was Khasim who had the portrait placed in that frame, and it was he who had the quotation carved beneath it. He loved her, you see, though he was never what you could call a mother's boy. He was proud of her beauty, and the way she could ride the Arab stallions. She could also hunt in the desert like the men, but always she was a woman.'

'A very beautiful one,' Diane said softly. 'You look like her, Morgana.'

'So, also, does Khasim about the eyes. You see it, Diane, so admit it. At least give him credit for something.'

'I don't deny that he's a striking man to look at—many Arabs are, aren't they? Your mother wore a charming wedding gown; that silk looks as fine as moonlight, and I like the way the veil is arranged so it reveals her dark hair.'

'We call such a veil a *chaddur*. Some Arabian brides overdo the cosmetics and allow themselves to be plastered in kohl and henna. It's a kind of fertility rite, but I don't care for it. When I marry Rauf I shall wear a simple dress with the *chaddur* and I hope to look just as she does. I have her necklace; Khasim gave it to me when I came of age. I said to him at the time that he should save it for his own bride, but he only smiled and placed it around my neck. I hope——'

Morgana drew a sigh and faced Diane. 'I sometimes wonder if Khasim will ever marry. The Beni-Haran expect him to do so, so he can have a son to carry on in his place, but he is now thirty-five and shows no sign of taking a bride——'

'There is always Hiriz.'

'There is—you.'

'What——?' Diane backed away from Morgana and her face seemed filled with her eyes, the dense sapphire blue they always became when she was disturbed. 'What are you saying?'

'You heard me.' Morgana lifted the lamp and played its tinted light over Diane's figure in the cashmere *jellaba*. 'You are young and healthy, and you challenge him as I have never seen a woman challenge him. You have in your veins the blood of soldiers, and you have the fine bones of good breeding. You would have with Khasim a fine and lusty son——'

'Please—please stop what you're saying!' Diane was trembling; her legs felt so unsteady that she felt as if she were going to fall down. 'Your brother is the last man on earth I should want to marry ... I am the last woman on earth he would want for a wife! We hate each other!'

'You say it so emphatically, as if to convince yourself that it's hate you feel for Khasim. Is it, Diane? Can you truly say that when you look at him you feel yourself shrinking inside that he should lay a finger upon you? There are men who affect women in that way, but can you honestly say that it disgusts you, the mere idea of feeling his mouth on your lips and his body pressed to yours?'

'I—I don't want to talk about such a thing——'

'Why?' Morgana insisted. 'Has life with an elderly

grandparent made you repressed? Do natural instincts make you feel ashamed?'

'No——'

'Are you certain, Diane? It seems to me that your life with your grandfather may have been more sheltered than mine has been. We Arab girls are taught very young what it means to be a woman, and Khasim was enlightened enough to allow me to be educated. Were you brought up more like a boy? I expect it would have pleased Colonel Ronay to have had a grandson so he could have joined the army and carried on the military tradition, but as things turned out he had a girl on his hands instead, and you told me yourself that you wore shirts and breeches most of the time and were taught boyish skills rather than feminine ones.'

'Grandpère and I were very close and I liked our life the way it was.' Tears filled Diane's eyes as it swept over her in a forlorn wave that the one caring person in her life was no longer alive to love her. She was alone in a world of strangers ... she glanced around her, a tear falling to her cheek as she searched for someone she could turn to in her lonely plight.

Something touched her and with a startled gasp she glanced downwards and there was an enormous Persian cat rubbing its furry body against her dress. She could hear the animal purring and bending down she stroked the handsome head and met the sheer green eyes. 'You beauty,' she murmured. 'Will you allow me to pick you up?'

'That's Pasha,' Morgana smiled. 'He won't object to being cuddled, but he's very heavy. He wanders about in the *kasbah* cellars and eats the mice, and as this is a very old building there are quite a colony of them down there.'

'I'm very fond of cats.' Diane lifted the big Persian into her arms and derived a certain comfort from his friendly warmth. He purred louder than the twin tabbies that lived in the stables at home ... Diane caught her breath, home had become a faraway house empty of its owner. Coco, her grandfather's servant, would have seen to the funeral, and he would doubtless be worried because she had failed to return for the burial. Coco knew the desert ... he would believe like others that she had fallen prey to its hot sun or its predators. He would remain at the house for a while, and then close it up and go and live with his brother Bertrand in Marseilles.

'Pasha likes you,' Morgana remarked. 'Come, let us go and have some supper. Bring the cat with you if you like—do you know what they say about people who have an affinity with cats?'

'I had heard,' Diane said offhandedly.

Morgana laughed. 'To be a sensuous person is nothing to be ashamed of—you are probably far more responsive than a girl like Hiriz, who shrieks and runs if Pasha so much as looks at her.'

'She probably doesn't like the idea of all the mice he has consumed.' Diane fondled his soft ears as she followed Morgana from the salon. They went to a smaller, much cosier room where supper was served to them. All the time they ate their meal, Selim stood on guard outside the door.

'How long,' Diane exclaimed, 'does your brother think he can keep me locked up in this—this Bluebeard's castle of his?'

Morgana ate creamy cheesecake and looked unconcerned. 'Come, have some of this delicious cake and stop being so anxious, and accept that you are here because it was meant to happen. *Mektub.*'

'Written in the sands—someone said that to me just before I came East.' Diane took a sip of dark sweet Arabian coffee. 'I wonder if Grandpère knew his days were numbered when I spoke to him of coming here and he made so few objections. He wanted me to see the desert, but he had grown too frail to come with me. He was frailer than I guessed and like an old soldier he wanted to die without any fuss ... I should have seen that, but I—I was too taken up with my travelling arrangements, and he seemed quite content when I left him. He was in the garden looking at his roses——'

Diane broke off huskily. Coco would have seen to it that there were roses on the coffin, and the sheathed sword whose shining steel had indicated the attack on the Beni-Haran.

'He did his duty as he saw it,' she said, swallowing back the tears. 'I can't condemn him when he was always loving and kind towards me.'

'That is the way of life,' Morgana agreed. 'We have to accept people for the way they are towards ourselves. There is no perfection and for most of the flaws in people there is a virtue that compensates. Each one of us is a little selfish and yet at times sacrificing; a little cruel but also kind. We are human beings, not angels.'

'Eastern wisdom?' Diane extended cream on her finger so Pasha could lick it off.

'Written in the sands, Diane, as you said yourself. The desert will still be here when we are dust, so accept life and what it brings you—it may be the romance you believe in.'

The cat's prickly tongue flicked its way around Diane's finger, and that night he slept on her bed. She lay awake for a while listening to the strains of Eastern music drifting through the mesh of her windows, the fine netting drawn around her bed to keep out insects. Though she heard no sound of a footfall outside her door she sensed a presence and supposed it was one of the guards. She hadn't been locked in, but she well knew that the big main gates of the *kasbah* were secured for the night.

Diane lay there in the aromatic darkness, the warm weight of Pasha against her curled-up legs ... she drew the silky bedcovers around her and remembered the feel of a cloak still warm from a powerful body. Strange feelings trembled through her own body and she lay wondering how she would cope with Kasim ben Haran when he decided to carry his threats to their ultimate conclusion.

He could be cruel, and yet at times strangely thoughtful. A mixture of cruelty and kindness were certainly blended in his blood and Diane could never be sure which side of his personality he would show her. Pasha purred contentedly in the darkness as Diane fell asleep ... wondering.

CHAPTER EIGHT

In the following days Diane saw very little of the Caid, but to her delighted astonishment she was allowed to visit the bazaar with his sister, the two of them swathed from head to ankles in the enveloping robes the women of Shemara wore when they ventured into the streets.

They spent quite some time in the shop of silks, and never had Diane seen and handled such gorgeous fabrics, a sensuous delight to the eye and the touch. Petal-fine silks, glimmering brocades, diaphanous chiffon and supple velvet, and lace that took away her breath with its exquisite detail. Whatever she admired was immediately ordered for delivery to the *kasbah*, her protests being waved away by Morgana. 'A sewing woman will come and make dresses for you. Arab women are good at simple styles with a pretty addition of lace or embroidery. Now we'll go and visit my little man who mixes such divine perfumes. Come!'

They went deep into the market place that teemed with life, colour and a variety of aromas. Beneath frayed palm-fibre awnings the stalls were laden with goods, and hot slivers of sunlight lanced down on faces whose shades of skin ranged from pale honey to deepest brown, set with startling eyes that gazed inquisitively into Diane's blue ones above the veiling across her face.

Here in the shadowy archways and lanes of the *kissaria* the robed figures mingled and bartered in the language that sounded so fierce, and the aroma of strong coffee came drifting from the doorways of the cafés mixing with the spicy smell of foodstuffs and the sweet tang of huge Jaffa oranges, ripe apricots and piles of figs, dates and grapes.

Precarious cage-like balconies hung from the sun-scaled walls of the old houses sloping along the alleyways, and the clinking cups of a lemonade seller blended with jangling camel bells and the braying of donkeys well laden with baskets and sometimes a rider whose slippers scraped the ground at each side of a flea-bitten back.

The *kissaria* was studded with small shops that sold a variety of handcrafts, for here the ancient crafts were carried on, the engraving of precious metals and the tooling of leather; the weaving of fine carpets and all kinds of blankets.

Towering above all was the prayer tower of the green-domed mosque, its minaret almost as fragile as petrified lace, its acorn-shaped doorways the perfect frames for the colourful scenes of Eastern life ... the inner life Diane had never really expected to see, both fascinating and fierce.

Morgana beckoned Diane to a shop doorway and told her that here the craftsmen were making bridal chests, which were of dark silky wood rich with an inlay of mother-of-pearl. The owner of the shop spoke to Morgana, who greeted his remark with a laugh. She explained to Diane that he wanted to know if he could provide either of them with such a chest.

'Well, Diane, shall I order one of them for you?' Morgana's dark eyes sparkled with amusement above the veiling that concealed her other features.

'No, thank you!' Diane walked on, and then gave a gasp as an Arab stepped into her path, the coils of a large snake wrapped about his neck. His eyes stared into hers and he had tiny scars all over his face. Suddenly he grinned and thrust the snake towards her so its flickering tongue was only inches from her face. Instantly one of the Caid's guards leapt forward to grab hold of the snake-charmer, who with the agility of a snake slid away into the crowd. The guard turned and stared intently at Diane, as if afraid that she had been bitten.

'Tell him I'm all right,' she said to Morgana. 'That awful snake man gave me a fright, that's all.'

Morgana reassured the guard, who gave Diane an apologetic bow and rejoined his companion.

'Had you been bitten,' Morgana remarked, 'that little beast would have been hunted down and had the hide flayed off him with a whip.'

Diane shivered. 'Was it a venomous snake?' she asked.

'Oh yes. The men who handle them become immune to the venom, but you saw his scars, didn't you?'

Diane nodded as they walked on, more than ever aware of the stares as she and Morgana made their way to the perfumery; she overheard remarks which she couldn't understand yet which were easy to interpret. She knew that she was being pointed out as the *roumia* who was staying at the *kasbah*.

'Your brother's very subtle, isn't he?' she said.

'What makes you say that, Diane?'

'He appears to give me the freedom of his city, but what would his guards do if I started to walk in the direction of the gates?'

Morgana merely smiled and paused in front of a little shop like a hole in the wall.

'My brother seems to be on your mind continually, Diane,' she spoke in a mock innocent voice. 'I'm betrothed to be married, but Rauf isn't always on my mind. Right this moment I look forward to having a new perfume blended for me—what kind would you like, *chérie*, one with a tang of leather, horses and tobacco smoke?'

'That isn't fair——' Diane looked indignant. 'I'm not always thinking about your high and mighty brother!'

'Aren't you?' Morgana laughed to herself as she entered the scent shop, pulling aside her veil and revealing her face as from the rear quarters of the shop a bearded and wizened Arab appeared, treating Morgana to a deep salaam and greetings in French.

'I bring with me a friend, Ahmar, to have blended for her a scent to suit her personality in your inimitable way.'

Ahmar gazed a moment at Diane and then politely requested that she draw aside her veil, and then extend to him her hand. Diane was only too glad to uncover her face, for she felt slightly absurd in a veil, as if she were dressed up for a musical comedy. She held out her hand and felt the Arab's bony fingers close around hers; her skin looked very white in contrast to his and she stifled a small protest when he raised her hand to his nostrils and sniffed at her skin.

'Merely a formality, *sitt*.' His deep-set eyes twinkled at her. 'I had heard a whisper that an English lady was staying at the Caid's palace—there is no place like a market place for the rapid exchange of news and you must forgive us if we find it intriguing that a young woman from overseas comes to stay among us. Have you yet formed an opinion of Shemara?'

'My friend has not yet seen very much of our city,' Morgana broke in. 'This is her first visit to the East and she still finds our ways a little strange.'

'Shemara is one of the oldest of desert cities, and at the same time just progressive enough to suit our way of life without spoiling it.' Ahmar gazed into Diane's eyes as if reading them. 'There are areas of the East which make progress too rapidly and they will be overcrowded slums in a few short years, uncared for by the sheiks who go elsewhere to live and invest. Shemara will not go uncared for while Khasim ben Haran holds the power, Allah preserve him.'

Diane just stood there, tongue-tied and unable to blurt out that Khasim ben Haran never did show his progressive side where she was concerned. Even if this shrewd old Arab suspected the truth, he seemed only too ready to accept the story that was being circulated around Shemara, that she was Morgana's guest at the *kasbah*.

'Now let us proceed with the blending.' Ahmar

pressed her hand and released it. 'Something cool and delicate for the *sitt*, with a dash of the sensuous, eh?'

For the next hour they were entertained in this way, watching as the deft old fingers mingled the fragrances of the East in various phials until he finally arrived at the aroma he required for each of them, when the perfumes were carefully poured into charming little bottles.

'Never purchase a scent in a large bottle,' he told Diane. 'Scent can be likened to love; it will evaporate if it isn't closely guarded. Now, *sitt*, you have your own special blend of scent that will mingle with the natural oils of your skin and produce in the man who breathes it a desire to keep you close to him—that is every woman's wish, is it not?'

Diane fondled the little bottle. 'Is it?' she parried. 'My scent has no name, so what do I call it?'

'I will write the label now.' Ahmar leaned over his work table and wrote a single Arabic word on a little, old-fashioned label with a surround of flowers. He handed it to her and she carefully moistened it and applied it to the bottle.

'Show me.' Morgana leaned over her shoulder to take a look. 'Mmm, very appropriate,' she murmured. 'Shall I translate for you?'

'I'll die of curiosity if you don't,' Diane rejoined. 'What does the word mean?'

'Enclosed garden.'

'Oh——'

'Aren't you pleased? To an Arab there is nothing more enticing than a garden within walls where the flowers and fountains are concealed from the outside world. Ahmar pays you an immense compliment, so do thank him.'

'*Merci.*' Diane smiled at the old man. 'I shall wear the scent only for special occasions.'

'There should be many special occasions for a young woman,' he replied. 'When we have our youth we should never waste it in the garden of cares, for they should be set aside for when we are older, wiser, more patient with the complexities of being human. For each of us there is a time of roses and honey, so walk in the garden of joy, *lalla*, and let the wings of your heart take flight.'

'It's the philosophy which helps us to arrive at old age with serenity.' He stroked his beard and stood watching them from the doorway of his tiny shop, veiled to the eyes once more and followed by the Caid's guards as they made their way back to the *kasbah*.

The scents of the shop lingered in Diane's nostrils, just as the words of the old Arab lingered in her mind. She couldn't deny that Shemara was a fascinating place, if only she were free to walk about in her own style of dress, without this veil which made her feel conspicuous instead of concealed. Was that the reason why Arabian girls liked to wear the *yashmak*, because it attracted the glances of men and made them wonder whether the face beneath the veil was lovely or plain?

'Why do you wear the veil, Morgana?' she asked. 'Everyone knows who you are——'

'That isn't the point, *chérie*.' Morgana's eyes were amused, and alluring above the veil. 'Nothing was ever invented that is more seductive than a mask of silk across a woman's face. The women of Europe should take it up, for along with our enveloping robes it isn't a sign of male oppression but of a jealous protectiveness on the part of the men. When women are taken for granted,

Diane, the sexual difference then takes on the quality of indifference.'

'More Eastern wisdom?' Diane's own eyes had a deep blue brilliance as they caught the sun, high over the prayer tower of the mosque where the noonday call to prayer echoed over the market-place. '*Haya alla Salat! Haya alla Falah!*'

It was a strange, rather moving sound, dying away into silence as the two girls crossed the courtyard of the *kasbah*. The inner fountain court was cooler, where masses of flowering vines mantled the walls and cloisters, and feathery green trees shaded a pool of fish.

Diane knelt on the tiled rim of the pool and watched the fish as they flickered through the water, their red-gold bodies almost transparent as they swam among the big-leaved water-lilies.

'You look rather like a contemplative nun,' Morgana remarked. 'Are your reflections nun-like?'

'That would hardly be possible in a place as sensual as the East.' Diane trailed her fingers in the pool and the inquisitive fish fluttered around them, prodding her skin to see if she might be eatable.

'I think you came to the East as trustingly as you put your fingers in that water,' Morgana said. 'What if my brother kept piranha in that pool?'

'I'd know by now, wouldn't I?' Diane smiled as she gazed down at the exotic fish with their tails like smoke. 'It never occurred to me that I'd meet a man like Khasim ben Haran in the desert.'

'But where else would you meet such as he?' Morgana's gaze dwelt upon the tall palm trees with their graceful fronds shading bushes of pomegranate, Persian lilac, poinsettias and the Barbary fig with its twisted branches. 'In my brother, Diane, is the desert. He's as much a part of it as the wild hawks that fly there, as the sand leopards and the *khamsin*. I wonder, did you obey the call of the sands, or did my brother's voice call your name?'

'He—he didn't know about me——' Diane sat as tense on the tiled rim as if turned to stone. 'As if such far-fetched things happen! I wanted to visit the East, and as Fetna is on the outskirts of your brother's land it isn't so strange that we—we met the way we did. You people are steeped in the idea that everything happens because of some devious design of fate. If my grandfather had been a lawyer or a farmer, then I wouldn't be here at all, would I?'

'No,' Morgana agreed. 'Nor would Khasim bear the scar of a Spahi sword. The pattern of our lives weaves itself from what happens to our parents. Had Philippe Ronay been a peaceful farmer then he would not have been responsible for making war on the Beni-Haran. For years Khasim has lived with the name of Ronay stamped on his mind, and I believe his thoughts travelled across the silent sands and drew you here.'

'He didn't know of my existence,' Diane protested. 'I—I've never seen anyone look so ferocious as he did when he discovered who I was. I thought he'd break my neck and I don't know what stopped him. I suppose that way would be too quick to satisfy him.'

'You have made up your mind about him, haven't you, Diane? But I wonder what is happening in your heart?'

'My heart aches for my grandfather.' Diane drew her gaze from Morgana and let it travel around the court of the seven fountains. 'No one will be allowed into this place to find me. Even your brother's own people believe he keeps women here, so the French are bound to respect the privacy of his harem. If they hear about my presence at the *kasbah* they're unlikely to believe that the Caid of Shemara has me here against my will. Women fall at his feet and revel in his power over them, but I'm not like them. Do you know what he said to me, Morgana? He told me that when I fall in love with him, he'll let me go.'

Diane drew her hand from the pool and the drops of water fell on to the sun-warmed rim and dried instantly. 'He'll never let me go back home to Brittany until I—I——'

'You could always pretend to love him,' Morgana said quietly. 'Why not behave with him like Hiriz if you really wish to leave Shemara? Make yourself tiresome. Twine your arms around him and press kisses to his scarred face. Fall at his feet, Diane Ronay, if that's the key that will set you free.'

'I—I couldn't.' Diane rose to her feet. 'I won't give him that kind of satisfaction.'

'Then he'll take it, Diane. Come, let us go and eat. Walking around the *kissaria* with its smells of food always gives me an appetite.' Morgana walked towards the arching entrance to the *kasbah* apartments, but Diane stood pensively beside the pool, thoughts milling in and out of her mind with the same rapidity as the fish in the water. Elusive if she tried to take hold of them and yet prodding her at their own volition.

She sighed as thoughts of Brittany entered her mind, the garden of the lonely house going to seed now Grandpère was no longer there, and dust gathering on the furniture, the books, the platoons of miniature troops on the baize-covered table in the den.

Brittany seemed far removed from this exotic garden where dragonflies flew on gauzy red wings beneath great archings of scented jasmine. Fountains splashed upon stone and turtle-doves strutted on the tilework and cooed in the sun, fanning out their white curly tails. Massive marigolds blended their gold with the ivory of oleanders, and harmal and henna mingled their perfume. Masses of lantana smothered one of the fountains and it seemed alive with butterflies, gorgeous as patterned silk, fragile as chiffon as they lifted and fell among the flowers.

Insects buzzed and sunlight lay over the courtyard like a silent tide of gold, glittering as it caught the specks of mica in the tiles. Slim-stemmed palms stood against the sky like green giants and jacaranda trees dripped with lilac-coloured flowers.

Diane's bemused gaze followed the flight of a gauzy dragonfly and she watched fascinated as it flew into a snare of jasmine and was lost among the cluttering creamy star-like petals.

She felt as if snared in a trap that was both beautiful and terrifying, and she watched breathlessly to see if the dragonfly would re-emerge. The seconds ticked by and became minutes and the dragonfly seemed hopelessly lost in the jasmine, perhaps overcome by the scent ... or unwilling to leave its prison.

Birds piped in a pepper tree and then went suddenly silent. A shadow hovered above the courtyard and then came swooping down on widely spread wings. Diane looked upwards and caught her breath as the great hawk swooped and circled her figure; she actually caught the whine of the air in its wing feathers as the bird came in to land on the stone rim of a nearby fountain. Its sharp eyes watched her and its talons gripped the stone and made a scraping sound as it shifted nearer to her. Instinctively she stood very still, feeling the heavy beat of her heart and the crawling of her skin as she imagined those talons tearing into her.

It was the Sheik's hawk, trained to kill its prey in the desert. She felt frightened and wanted to run for cover, but knew that if she moved the hawk would react to her movement and perhaps attack her.

'That's it,' a voice said, the timbre of it passing along her nerves like a touch. 'Stay very still ... it's your hair, *chérie*, it caught his eye in the sunlight, sheeny gold as a sunbird's plumage.'

He came across the fountain court, his hand in its leather gauntlet held out to the hawk. From his lips came the whistle of command, and Diane held her breath as the big hunting bird shifted its gaze from her to its master, the great wings spreading out, speckled like tortoiseshell and casting shadows in the sun. The Sheik spoke in Arabic to the hawk and to Diane's amazement the predatory bird cocked its head rather in the manner of a pet macaw. Gripping the fountain rim with its talons it strutted along the stone until it was close enough to rub its head against the man's shoulder.

'Love is curious, is it not?' The Sheik spoke in French to Diane. 'It's there in the hearts of the fiercest of creatures and perhaps is all the more precious if it beats in a wild heart rather than a tame one. Strange, but I also found Malik in the desert. He was a fledgling then and had somehow hurt a wing. Even then he would have pecked out my eyes if he could have got at them; as it was, my hand was badly bloodied by the time I got him to my tent. I set the wing and he mended rapidly. Cautiously he accepted my attentions and took to me, but even to this day my men steer clear of him. He's very powerful and temperamental—you were wise, Diane, to stand your ground. Had you tried to run, he would have gone for you.'

All the time he spoke the Sheik kept his eyes on the

hawk and didn't glance once at her. He spoke again in Arabic and with a single powerful movement of the beautiful wings the hawk flew to the leather gauntlet and settled upon it.

'Stay as you are, Diane.' The Sheik spoke softly. 'Malik may still fancy those blue eyes of yours, so I will take him to the stables where he has his perch. You will remain here until I return!'

She rebelliously told herself that she wouldn't and as the cloaked figure strode off with the hawk, Diane took a step towards the house. '*Mon dieu——!*' Her knees almost buckled beneath her and she sagged against a palm tree and leaned against the plaited trunk. This was ridiculous—a reaction, no doubt, to standing still while the hawk held her at bay. Her fingers gripped the rough fibres of the tree as the Sheik reappeared, blue-cloaked, a white headrobe framing his lean brown face and the half-hooded eyes that seemed to her as dangerously intent as the hawk's had been.

He loomed over her, his eyes consuming her in their darkness, noticing how she clung to the palm tree. A smile twitched briefly at the very edge of his mouth.

'You can stop being afraid,' he said softly. 'You are going home where you belong ... the house of the hawk is no place for the dove.'

Diane gazed up at the Sheik, unaware that her eyes reflected the blueness of the sky where the sun burned high like a white flame. The sun-darkened face had a look of tension, and suddenly there was a splintering crack as the shaft of his whip broke in his hands. He flung the pieces from him, almost with anger. 'Did you hear what I said, girl? I shall ride with you to Dar-Arisi and from there you can take the boat that will carry you home to Brittany.'

'Home?' The word came huskily from her lips ... that dark shuttered house where in the silence the only sound was the ticking of the panelled clock in the hall. The door of the den was closed; the big winged chair was empty.

'Yes, and this time I shall ride with you in the desert to ensure that you arrive safely at the hotel. We'll set out when the sun goes down. It's better to travel when the sands have cooled for the day, and tonight there will be a moon to light the way.'

'Why are you doing this?' A hand had climbed to her throat as if to relieve its constriction.

'It's what you want, Diane.'

'It was never your policy, Sheik Khasim, to give me what I want.'

'I have changed my policy.' He spoke almost brusquely. 'A man may do that, mayn't he? The debt between Ronay and myself is discharged—it was wrong of me to expect you to pay.'

Diane leaned there against the tree; her legs were trembling and deep inside she felt weak when she looked at the strong cloaked shoulders and let her eyes travel upwards to the scar that clawed his flesh and bone. Suddenly there was no way to stop her hand from reaching out so she could tentatively stroke his face.

He stood very still, and then a groan broke from his lips. 'I warn you, Diane—I have only sufficient self-control to escort you to Dar-Arisi, so take your hand away before I have none left.'

'It's such a deep scar,' she murmured. 'No wonder it held so much bitterness. Like the hawk you wanted to tear me apart, didn't you?'

'Yes.' In a kind of rage he reached out and his hands gripped her shoulders; his eyes blazed down into hers and his face was savage. 'I meant every cruel word I ever said to you, but each time I was cruel I wanted to caress you until you moaned with love and longing in my arms. Each night you have been here at the *kasbah* I have guarded your door myself, and all but needed guards to keep me from coming into you. The time has come for you to go, Diane. You make me vulnerable. You make me aware of loneliness. You move my heart strangely. I make yours beat fast with fear.'

Yes, her heart was beating fast, but where was the fear? What she felt was a kind of exhilaration ... was it because he had said he would take her to Dar-Arisi so she could go home to Brittany? She explored the thought and found it as bleak as a house without lights in the windows. She envisaged saying goodbye to Khasim ben Haran ... her Arab captor.

'No——' The word broke from her. 'I couldn't bear it!'

'So,' he agreed. 'I have said you can leave. I shall ride with you in order to be sure you arrive safely——'

'I don't want to leave!' She pressed her face against him and she was trembling all over ... an excited kind of trembling, such as she had felt the morning she had set out for Fetna and had ridden into the desert for the first time, into the absolute stillness and emptiness, both terrifying and wonderful. With loping strides her horse had carried her across the ridges of rough-pelted sand, and perhaps she had known then that she was riding away for always from the sheltered life into realms of danger ... romance ... the city of Shemara.

City of shadows and shutters, of strange little shops deep in the shade of weathered stone, pungent with the spices of the East. A city fed and cooled by the great plantation of date trees, towering, arching, or twisting their trunks in and out like those of affectionate elephants.

'Do you realise what you're saying?' The Sheik gripped her by the nape of the neck and tilted her head so her eyes were naked under his gaze. He searched them unsparingly. 'I am an Arab, Diane. Give yourself to me and you will be my exclusive property, every inch and hair of you. Do you understand? Do you comprehend my kind of love? Do you, my girl?'

'If I had the nerve to stand up to your hate, then I should be able to stand up to your—love.' She spoke the word hesitantly, still unsure of all it meant in relation to this man ... her grandfather's most bitter enemy.

'It isn't in a standing position that I envisage you, *bint*.' With a smile laced with wickedness he swept her up in his arms and carried her towards the *kasbah*.

'Khasim!' She struggled, but only slightly. 'Perhaps, after all, I should go back to Brittany——'

He checked his striding and stood there with his arms holding her locked to him. 'Don't play games with me, Diane. Stay or go, but let it be one or the other!'

She laid her head against his shoulder and the scents of him were in her nostrils—horses, leather and *cigarro* smoke. They had become familiar, but still his true intentions confused her and stirred some fire beneath the ashes of her fear.

'Am I to be your—your *kadine*?' she breathed into the side of his warm neck, unevenly, fearing his answer but needing to hear it.

'My *what*?' he roared, stirring a string of doves into flight from the stone rim of the archway. 'By Allah, you and I will lack communication in all places but the one! I mean to marry you, girl. I took it for granted you under-

stood me——' His eyes flashed down to meet hers, penetrating their blueness until, growling her name, he bent
his head and took her lips with his, crushing them and
combining bliss with pain.

'By Allah, there will be opposition,' he told her, his lips
travelling back and forth across her eyes. 'My people
expect me to marry a woman of the Beni-Haran, and
now starts the business of making them understand that
they have my loyalty, my life, but I need to have my
roumia. It was written! I knew that day I found you half
dead in the desert. You were Ronay's last link with life
and you came to me across the water, across the sands,
and it was almost as if he sent you to me. I shall have
you for my own, Diane, and the Beni-Haran will have to
learn to accept you—it might take close on a year, but it
will happen.'

'A year?' Diane held him about the neck and it was
beginning to seep into her senses and her very bones that
he liked her to touch him. His eyelids grew sensuously
heavy when she did so, and his lashes were so black and
thick against his tawny skin that to look at him made
her feel as if her insides were melting.

'We may be fortunate and it may take only nine
months from the night that we marry,' he murmured.

'Khasim!'

'Let's make it a son, my *bint*, and my people will find
you as irresistible as I do.'

'Khasim——' His name died away under the onslaught
of his kiss, and overhead the doves fluttered back to their
perch on the arching stone entrance into the *kasbah* of
the Caid.

**Harlequin brings you
a book to cherish ...**

three stories of
love and romance
by one of your
favorite
Harlequin authors ...

JOY
ROMANCE
LOVE

Harlequin Omnibus

THREE love stories in ONE beautiful volume

The joys of being in love...
the wonder of romance...
the happiness that true love brings...

Now yours in the HARLEQUIN OMNIBUS
edition every month wherever
paperbacks are sold.